# CHASED

## M. Liz Boyle

M. Liz Boyle

# CONTENTS

# CHAPTER 1

"You know how for years my favorite hobby was making Ellie scream?" Sawyer asked me through our webcam chat. I was surprised that he wanted to talk to me, but apparently he needed advice about Ellie. Not that I was sure what made me an expert, but hey, I was glad to hear the inside scoop on two of my favorite people. My older sister Ellie and our family friends' son Sawyer used to be rivals, but lately they'd been getting along *very* well.

I couldn't help but giggle. "You mean like the time you put worms in her water bottle? Or when you wrangled a garter snake into her hiking boot just before she tried to put on her boots?"

Sawyer laughed as he remembered. "That was golden. She was so mad at me, and the veins in her forehead bulged out so far, I thought she was going to have a stroke." It was funny – afterward, I mean. At the time, Ellie was so furious I didn't dare laugh. Sawyer and Marshall were laughing, even when their dad, Mr. Caleb, gruffly told Sawyer to have some respect.

That's when Sawyer said, "You're right, Dad. I was wrong to tamper with nature. I'll put the snake back where I found it." Mr. Caleb looked exasperated and embarrassed, Marshall laughed again, and Ellie tossed the confused and probably dizzy snake at Sawyer and stomped off to our tent. Sawyer had matured a lot since then, but I was wondering where the conversation was going.

"Yeah, so what's up?" I prodded.

"Before I forget," he interjected, "if Ellie comes into the room, hang up."

"Oh-kay. So what's up?" *Could we just get on with this?!*

"Well, do you remember the first time she laughed at one of my jokes?"

*Um, no.* It wasn't a memory I recalled daily, but I didn't want to say that. "Was it the time..." I let my voice trail off, hoping he would fill in the blank, which he did.

"Yeah, it was the time in Washington when we stopped for lunch and Lydie asked me if I would play grocery store with her. I wasn't exactly daydreaming of playing grocery store when there were amazing mountains and streams to explore, but when the cutest little kid in the world asks, you'll do almost anything." Lydie had been a super cute little kid. Now, at twelve, she's getting so she looks pretty more than cute, but I knew what Sawyer meant.

"So I gathered up rocks and pinecones and stuff for her to ring up," Sawyer recalled, "and when she grabbed a particularly big leaf, she asked if I wanted my milk in a bag. I told her she could leave it in the carton. Lydie just smiled and handed me my nature purchases, but Ellie laughed. Like she really thought I made a funny joke. It wasn't like the time Marshall watched a video on cutting hair and completely botched up mine. That time her laugh was like, 'What were you thinking?!' When I joked with Lydie that day, Ellie laughed like my joke actually made her happy." Even through the laptop screen, I could see Sawyer's face light up when he thought about Ellie smiling. And that made me smile. To be totally honest, when Ellie smiles it makes me happy too.

Now that he mentioned it, I did remember him making Ellie laugh that time in Washington. I also *definitely* remembered the bad haircut. I was glad his tousled, sandy-colored hair had made a strong comeback.

"Yeah, Sawyer, of course Ellie laughed. It was a really good joke." I was getting impatient to find out what was on Sawyer's mind.

"Hey, man," I heard another guy's voice behind Sawyer. *Great, nothing like an untimely interruption.*

A well-muscled, well-dressed guy with brown skin and short, remarkably tidy dreadlocks filled the corner of the laptop screen, and Sawyer stood to talk to him. "Lowry, man," Sawyer smiled as he shook his hand.

"Sawyer, Willow is ready to drive me to the airport. I'll be back with Grandpa and my mom in Tennessee for two weeks and then I'm off to the Alps for my internship," the guy said with a southern-Appalachian accent.

"JJ Lowry, I'm a little jealous of your amazing summer plans. Take tons of pictures and notes for me," Sawyer said as they bumped knuckles. "And tell your grandpa and mom I said 'hey.'"

"Right on, Dude," JJ Lowry said. "And I'll put in a good word, so you can make it into the Alps internship next year. Enjoy Montana and Ellie," he said with a grin. Then noticing Sawyer's computer, he quickly said, "Oh, really sorry I interrupted. Wait, that's not Ellie!" He looked perplexed.

"It's her sister."

JJ cocked an eyebrow, looking confused. I tentatively waved. I felt like a fly on the wall, except a thousand miles away. He peered around Sawyer's shoulder and waved back to me, with his left eyebrow peaked in confusion the whole time.

"I need to ask Marlee how to break the news to Ellie," Sawyer said, making me feel even more puzzled – and worried.

JJ's eyes grew and his mouth made an O. Patting Sawyer's shoulder he said, "Good luck. Keep me posted. See you in three months, Roomie." He waved to me, and I waved back uncomfortably. Sawyer bid him farewell and turned back to me.

"Sorry, Marlee. Okay, so that day when I made Ellie laugh, something changed. I loved hearing her laugh. I loved that I made her laugh. It completely changed my attitude toward Ellie."

"You fell in love that day?" I teased. They were about fourteen or fifteen that summer, so I didn't really mean it. Not completely – I just wanted to see his reaction.

He tilted his head. "Mm, I think maybe the spark started that day. Love has to grow over time, you know?"

I just nodded. I didn't really know from personal experience, but Mom and Dad had explained love similarly to me before.

Sawyer said, "So the spark ignited, and from that point on, all I could think about was fanning the flames." Coming from Sawyer, I totally pictured him lighting a campfire with that metaphor. *So what news does he have to tell Ellie? Dude, hurry up!* I wanted to grab his shoulders and tell him to spill it. I clutched the sides of the laptop screen.

"Go on, Sawyer." I sounded impatient now.

"Okay," his voice started to sound nervous, "so you probably know that Ellie applied for a wildlife vet tech program here in Idaho?" It's all I'd heard about for two months, so I gave an affirmative nod.

"Sawyer," a lady's voice interrupted in the background. Sawyer rolled his eyes and quickly apologized to me before stepping back to open his dorm room door. I knew that at the Professional Outdoor Guides School, or POGS, the students spent about half their time in a dorm and half their time living and learning in the outdoors. It sounded amazing, and I was happy for Sawyer that he had the opportunity. He had found his niche in the outdoors, and I had no doubt he would be an excellent guide. But suddenly my attention was acutely focused on the attractive young woman on the screen. She looked around the same age as Sawyer and Ellie, about eighteen or nineteen, and had curly auburn hair.

"Hey, Acadia," Sawyer politely welcomed her, stepping directly in front of the screen. *Thanks for blocking my view. He totally did that on purpose. And is she seriously named after a national park?*

"I couldn't leave without saying goodbye to you, Sawyer," Acadia purred. *What's going on here? Do you two have a deep relationship for her to talk to you like that?* I was beginning to get suspicious.

"Uh, thanks for stopping by," Sawyer replied, sounding uneasy. "I still have my Cold Water Rescue test in the morning, and then will head out for my summer of backpacking and working at the climbing gym." That all matched what Ellie had said. But I hadn't heard about Acadia. Could she be the news? Better *not* be!

"Be safe, Sawyer. No free solo climbing, and be careful when you're bicycling across the country." Okay, I hadn't heard about Sawyer bicycling across the country. Maybe there was a lot of news to break to Ellie. And I didn't like the way Acadia was hovering over him like a mother hen – or a possessive girlfriend!

"Of course," Sawyer assured her.

"And keep posting on your blog; I can't get enough of your stories, Sawyer." *That's a little creepy.* For his creative writing class, Sawyer was required to start a blog. I knew Ellie followed SMiles on the Trail, and I had read a few of his posts, but I don't think Ellie would say that she *couldn't get enough of his stories*. I decided I didn't like Acadia very much. Acadia the girl, not the national park. Even though I'd never been to Acadia National Park, I'd always heard that it's an amazing place. But this Acadia seemed like a flirt, and I sure hoped she wasn't the news.

After she *finally* left, Sawyer returned his attention to our conversation. "I'm so sorry, Marlee. It's a busy week at POGS with students finishing up and moving out for summer." He looked really embarrassed and I think he could tell I was unnerved by Acadia.

"*Saw-yer*, what news do you need to break to Ellie?" I couldn't stand the suspense and didn't want to endure another interruption.

"What? Did you say my name?" Ellie asked as she walked into the living room. *Ugh.* I immediately closed the tab with Sawyer and pretended to type on my final essay for Literature Class. "Ode to Ellie. She's the best sister, and is rarely smelly," I rambled when Ellie's questioning eyes landed on my face. She looked totally unconvinced that I was actually working on an ode, but she didn't question what I had really said before she rolled her eyes, sighed softly, and returned to the kitchen.

It looked like I'd be smothered with suspense for another week before we would be hiking with the Miles family. Maybe between our back-to-back trips with them in Colorado and then in Montana, I could corner Sawyer and get it out of him.

# CHAPTER 2

I nearly walked right past the guy. If it hadn't been for Sawyer stopping our group and asking him if he was alright, I would've hiked past with a simple "hello" and figured he was taking a break. Sawyer was right to be concerned though, the way he sat on the small boulder with his head in his hands.

"You have enough water?" Sawyer asked.

He took a moment to look up and acknowledge us, so Sawyer squatted to look at him at eye level, and again asked, "Hey, are you all right?"

His face was flushed, and his eyes looked confused, as if he couldn't quite say what he was thinking. "Uh, yeah, man, just taking a break," he finally answered.

"We'll break with you. This looks like a good spot to rest," Sawyer said, gesturing to us to drop our packs. I didn't understand why we were stopping with a tired stranger, but I knew to trust Sawyer as our guide. The five of us removed our packs, although we weren't quick to grab snacks since we'd just taken a break less than ten minutes ago.

One of the requirements for Sawyer's program at POGS was to lead several different treks in varying locations. After sharing his itinerary with our parents and the local rangers, my parents agreed to let Ellie, Lydie, and I join Sawyer and his brother Marshall on this trip in Montana. It'd been just one year since our adventure in an avalanche. My parents, Forrest and Quinn, and Sawyer and Marshall's parents, Mr. Caleb and Ms. Julia, acknowledged that the avalanche was a freak natural disaster, and so they agreed to Sawyer's plan this summer. Obviously, they sternly warned each of us, especially Sawyer, that there were to be no surprises. We were to stick to the plan and do nothing foolish. I get why they warned us so firmly, but I also knew that we all learned our lesson from the avalanche. We didn't need to be told not to do anything foolish. With this fresh-slate opportunity, we all seemed to have the primary goal of strengthening the trust that had been dampened last summer.

What a summer it had been already. A week after Sawyer and I attempted to have our webcam conversation, our family met the Miles family at the base camp where we started last year – last year's peak, the location of the avalanche. It was phenomenal. Make that PHENOM-ENAL!!!

We had a dream-come-true trip and finally made it to the magnificent peak. Of course we were scared to attempt the same peak early in the summer, when it was still covered in snow. Believe me, none of us were asking for a second snowy ride down the mountain.

However, Dad and Mr. Caleb wanted to train Sawyer in leading on a snowy peak. While it was unnerving to hike the same trail that led us into the path of the massive avalanche previously, I think we had to do it to overcome our fear. We had unfinished business, so to speak, on that mountain. And the view and the sense of accomplishment were completely worth the risk. Once we finally made it up the mountain we had dreamed of (and occasionally had nightmares of), we felt triumphant. It was more than the view from the peak, even though that was awesome. It was even more than overcoming what almost killed us. It was about not being restrained by our fear. It was about keeping our eyes on the summit even when our memories were issuing red-flag warnings. It was about choosing strength rather than fear. I mean, it's not like we were going to throw caution to the wind and chalk it up to strength and courage (we learned that lesson), but we knew the risk we were taking and chose to be strong and face our fear.

After returning to base camp in Colorado, we had just enough time to rinse our clothes in the creek to prepare for the car trip with our parents north to Montana. The two-day drive was a nice opportunity to rest, although sitting in a car after hiking for a week does not make for happy muscles. We were very sore when we arrived at the trailhead in Montana – just in time to start hiking on the day that Sawyer's backcountry permit allowed.

Sawyer, eighteen-years-old and leading trips to earn his certificate, was officially our leader. Last week in Colorado, our dads were still technically co-guides, although they did give Sawyer many opportunities to act as the head leader. This week though, our parents would be base-camping about five miles away from the peak we planned to summit. Dad and Mr. Caleb wanted to be nearby in case we needed help. We had a new satellite messenger just in case. And Marshall was thankful not to be carrying it this time. Poor guy – he was still embarrassed about losing his backpack full of gear in the avalanche last summer. He had mowed lots of lawns, shoveled lots of snow, and done plenty of odd jobs to afford his new gear.

With Sawyer officially leading and advising us to take a break by the stranger, I dropped my backpack near the guy and slowly reached for a salty snack – for show more than anything, since I wasn't hungry. My sister Ellie sat near Sawyer and asked the guy his name. It took him a few seconds to answer, but he said, "Thad."

"How many miles have you done today, Thad?" Sawyer politely inquired. "We've gone six, and we're eager to pull into camp in just two more miles. My name's Sawyer."

Thad nodded, and said, "I have seven miles ahead of me."

*Seven miles left? It's already two in the afternoon!* Most backpackers try to be in camp about four o'clock so they can set up a good campsite, filter water, and prepare supper before sundown. I considered this, and I could see the shock in Sawyer and Ellie's eyes, but Sawyer maintained a neutral expression toward Thad. Ellie looked back at Lydie, Marshall, and me with a skeptical look and a quirked eyebrow. Marshall frowned, but Lydie appeared to be so busy reorganizing her pack not to have noticed the conversation at all. We didn't understand how Thad was going to hike seven *more* miles. Either he was very unknowledgeable, or unrealistically optimistic, or a little delirious from heat exhaustion.

"Whew," Sawyer whistled, sounding impressed. "Well, have some water and electrolytes with us before you keep going. Why are you doing so much in one day?"

Thad's eyes darkened, but he quickly shrugged nonchalantly. "Training. I'm an endurance athlete, training for the hundred-mile race in the mountains."

"Wow, good for you." Sawyer sounded positive and friendly, but I, knowing him pretty well, detected a hint of skepticism in his voice. It seemed like he didn't believe everything Thad was saying, but he was being polite while trying to gather information. And it was becoming apparent that Thad was overheated. While we snacked and sipped water, he just sat listlessly.

Finally Ellie held out a bag of gorp, the common nickname for "good old raisins and peanuts," to Thad, "Here," she offered. Thad hesitated, but did accept a handful. I noticed Sawyer and Ellie exchange a concerned look, like they had detected far more than Marshall, Lydie, or I had. Suddenly Thad stopped eating the nuts and put his hands on his knees, his face white. It looked like he was going to be sick, and I had no clue what to do other than back away. If he started dry-heaving, I wanted to get out of there.

Dad had told me about the signs of heat-related illness, but since I hadn't experienced it or seen someone with it, I couldn't remember all the symptoms. I figured that Thad was overheated though, because it sure had been hot the last few hours, and the one water bottle on the outside of his pack was empty. And he hadn't taken a drink since we'd been with him.

Sawyer gestured toward Thad's empty bottle, and holding out his own nearly full bottle, asked, "Mind if I fill you up?" Thad murmured a response, so Sawyer poured a whole liter into Thad's bottle. We'd filtered water at the last stream crossing, about a mile ago, so we had enough to share until the next water crossing.

Then Sawyer dug in his pack for a moment and pulled out his spare t-shirt. Soaking it in water from another bottle, he gently wrapped the wet shirt on Thad's head. Then I knew that Thad was definitely overheated. Without a word, Sawyer reached for Thad's wrist and stared at his watch. After a long minute, Sawyer cleared his throat and then politely said, "Thad, you have heat exhaustion. I'd like to stay with you for a few hours to make sure you regain your strength. Sound good?"

Thad looked dull and just nodded. *What does this mean for us? We're just going to ditch our itinerary to sit and wait with a total stranger for his body temperature to lower?* Suddenly, pricked by conscience, I became aware of my selfishness. Here I had been treating Thad like I was the priest or the Levite in the parable of the good Samaritan, but just one year ago, we were in a desperate situation and needed help. We would've jumped for joy if a group of five experienced backpackers stumbled upon us and offered to help. Here was our chance to practice genuine kindness. Lydie's recent memory verse popped into my mind. For a week she went around the house singing, "Do not forget to entertain strangers, for by doing so some have unwittingly entertained angels." Yikes! *God, please soften my heart!* Thad was a human too, made in God's image. I needed to treat him like that.

*Wow,* I thought, my attitude changing, *we might actually get to help someone. Really make a positive impact on Thad's trip. Maybe even save his life, depending on how serious his heat exhaustion is.* I was still nervous about how to help him, but I would try to be more joyful to do what I could and work with my tightly-knit group to help Thad.

Sawyer's voice interrupted my thought process. "Marsh, please come sit by Thad for a minute while I talk to Ellie. Try to get him to sip his water." Over the years, Sawyer and Ellie had been friendly rivals – well, maybe archenemies was a more fitting term – but during the avalanche adventure, their friendship had solidified into a genuine admiration for each other, first as friends, but then as something more. In the last year, they had talked on the phone several times a week or as often as Sawyer had phone service, depending on where he was. It was clear that they were content with the direction their relationship was going. I sure was. Marshall usually teased me for thinking they were cute together, but he couldn't deny it. But right now, I knew their quiet talk up the trail forty feet was about Thad and not each other. This was definitely not when Sawyer would break some mysterious news to Ellie, so I didn't sneak over to eavesdrop.

Marshall shot Lydie and me a helpless look as he opened Thad's water bottle and tried to interest him in it. Lydie stifled a giggle, and I knew exactly why. Marshall doesn't always have the most refined people skills, and usually he prefers to keep mostly to himself rather than initiate conversation. On the other hand, he and I had gotten to know each other much better on the avalanche trip. Knowing more about him made me feel guilty about laughing at his efforts. And in Marshall's defense, Dad has said that when people have heat exhaustion, they usually are confused. *Ha! I did remember something about heat exhaustion.* It would be difficult for *anyone* to convince Thad to drink at that point. Poor Marshall!

A couple minutes later, Sawyer and Ellie returned to us and sat down on the trail, so that we were all sitting in a sort of semi-circle, with Thad facing our group. Sawyer nodded at all of us, and with a quick smile from Ellie, Sawyer said, "Thad, like I said before, you have heat exhaustion. I'm currently training to be a professional mountaineering guide, so we're in a position where we can help you. Ellie here," Sawyer placed his hand on her shoulder, "has a decent amount of healthcare knowledge." It was probably good that Sawyer didn't specify that she's working on becoming a vet tech. Even though human healthcare is surprisingly similar to animal healthcare, according to Ellie, it tends to throw people off when she offers to help people while telling about her experiences at the vet clinic. Sawyer continued, "We'd like you to join our group until you get your strength back." At his conclusion, he looked between Marshall, Lydie and me, waiting for our affirming nods.

Thad would join our group. A complete stranger was now a temporary member of our close-knit group. *Don't be selfish, don't be selfish. Treat him like a brother, Marlee.* Sawyer's hand was still on Ellie's shoulder, and he gave it a gentle squeeze, prompting her to step forward.

Ellie is a beautiful, intelligent young lady who "strives for perfection," as Dad always says. Lydie and I have teased that 'strives for perfection' is the kind way of saying "an impossible-to-please perfectionist." But Ellie has matured so much in the past few years, and is learning to, in Mom's words, "settle for excellence."

Ellie stepped toward Thad and took Marshall's place, who happily gave up holding Thad's untouched water bottle. Ellie introduced herself to Thad, who at least looked up and acknowledged her. Marshall hadn't received so much as a nod. Holding the water bottle toward Thad's mouth, she politely but firmly said, "I need you to take a swallow, Thad." He swallowed a decent gulp of water. "Good, that's a good start," Ellie encouraged him. She glanced at her watch and reached for more gorp. Thad's eyes lit up a bit as she handed him the snack. "Start slow, just a few at a time. We don't need any throwing up," she said. He smiled at Ellie, and she innocently smiled back. I suddenly became aware of Sawyer behind me, and he instantly returned to Ellie's side.

I wondered if it made him jealous, the way Ellie was sitting near Thad. I wouldn't know. I really didn't have a crush on anyone – currently. I mean, sure I'd had crushes before, but most guys I knew were pretty immature still, and Marshall seemed like a brother, not a potential boyfriend. For now, I preferred just being good friends.

"I knew she'd do wonders," Sawyer said to Thad, obviously intending his praise to indicate *his* admiration for Ellie.

"Yeah," Thad said with a weird smile at Ellie. This clearly annoyed Sawyer, but Ellie still seemed completely oblivious to the way Thad was looking at her. I thought it was kind of creepy.

Twelve-year-old Lydie has always had a knack at breaking tension like this, and true to her character, she quickly said, "Well, Thad, tell us your life story. What brings you here? And why now? My name's Lydie, by the way. Short for Lydia. Is Thad short for anything?"

Sawyer, although thankful for the change in subject, interrupted. "We'll have time to get to know Thad as the evening goes on, but for now he needs to conserve his energy. Keep eating, man," Sawyer said, stepping between Thad and Ellie. "We'll take all the time we need for you to regain your strength before we go on to our campsite for the night."

"We should probably re-soak the t-shirt on his head, Sawyer," Ellie politely decided. "And it's time for another sip of water." Thad looked like he enjoyed Ellie's care. It looked like she was proud to be deemed the nurse of our group, and she was handling the role like a pro, but she seemed totally unaware of Thad's weird smiles and admiration. Sawyer looked proud of Ellie, but he seemed to be torn between helping Thad and sharing Ellie's kind attention with another guy – especially this guy. As for me, I definitely felt torn between helping this stranger and sticking to our planned adventure.

# CHAPTER 3

Over the next two hours, Thad recovered well. Sitting up tall, answering our questions with ease, and cheerily eating snacks and drinking water, he didn't even look like the same guy we had first encountered. In conversation, we learned that Thad is a local, Montana-born and raised and he has a deep connection with the trails in this area. He doesn't even need a map, but he likes learning about cartography, so he carries maps and blank maps and tries to fill in the locations and trails he hikes. That part sounded pretty cool.

Thad said he's twenty-four, a bachelor, and works on a maintenance crew at a local state park. While he didn't seem thrilled with the small talk, Thad did answer all our questions, but what grabbed my attention was the number of questions he asked *us*. Especially about where we were headed. He wanted to know exactly where we planned to hike, which days, what time of day, where we planned to camp, where we'd filter water, what sights we'd explore off-trail, exactly what type of gear we had along, and even why we chose to hike in that forest. He adamantly asked the *exact* location where we'd be camping that night, and even tried to convince us to camp somewhere else. His questioning was extensive, and it kind of made me feel like we were being interrogated. I wondered what we had done wrong. Honestly, I felt really unsettled the way he demanded our full itinerary.

Sawyer handled it pretty well, considering he was a lot younger, but part of me feared that Sawyer gave Thad too much information about our plans. Sawyer did try to change the subject or not-exactly answer some of Thad's questions, but Thad would just keep asking us in different wording until he got the information he wanted, and Sawyer was just too nice to politely tell him to mind his own business. Overall, Thad seemed okay, though. I didn't get the impression that he would hurt anyone, but he seemed very suspicious of us. Was he afraid we were going to hurt him? Did he feel a need to know our plans so he could escape from us if we turned evil? And what's more, he looked nervous when Sawyer said he could camp with us tonight. Not nervous as in, "I shouldn't impose on your group," but more like, "I want to camp anywhere in these woods except with your group." I wondered what he thought we would do to him. He even said he felt so much better that we could go on alone, but how could we leave him when he was so short on water?

The other thing about Thad that jumped out at me during our conversation was how he watched Ellie like a puppy gazes at its owner. And I'm certain that Ellie, and maybe Lydie, are the only ones who didn't notice. Sawyer looked jealous and really irritated, but Thad hadn't actually said or done anything disrespectful to Ellie, so he didn't have a real reason to say anything to Thad about it.

And besides, while Sawyer and Ellie are close friends who might be headed toward dating and marriage someday, they don't consider each other officially boyfriend and girlfriend yet, so what could Sawyer say to discourage Thad's puppy dog eyes for my sister? *"Hey, man, I see you're digging my best friend Ellie, and, well, you need to stop, because I've secretly had my eyes on her for the last half-decade, and I have plans to date her."* It would probably cause a fight. It was probably best that Sawyer kept quiet, although I wondered how long he'd watch Thad try to flirt with the still-oblivious Ellie and keep quiet.

Ellie is so smart most of the time, but I never knew she was more naive than I was. She thought she was just being a watchful nurse and that Thad was appreciative of her care. I was curious, albeit nervous, to see how the conflict would evolve.

Before I could wonder too long what would happen between Thad and Sawyer, Marshall nudged me with his elbow. "Hmm?" I asked.

Marshall nodded toward Thad. "Sawyer just said in three minutes we'll load up and move on toward our campsite. Pee now or hold it for two hours," he teased. I returned his grin. "What were you daydreaming about anyway?" he asked me.

As I stood to stretch, I felt my cheeks blush, realizing that I had been imagining a big confrontation between our beloved Sawyer and this mysterious Thad. "Uh," I stammered.

Marshall, so much more comfortable joking with me since the avalanche adventure, arched his eyebrows and said with mock surprise, "You were daydreaming about me? I'm touched, Marlee."

I laughed. What a goofball. I playfully punched his shoulder, and he challenged me to arm-wrestle. It might sound weird that I actually arm-wrestled with Marshall in the middle of the mountains with Thad in our group, but we're so much like family, except for the suspicious stranger, that I didn't think twice. I really wondered if I could beat him. I knew that Marshall was considerably stronger than I am in a lot of areas, but hey, I couldn't go down without a fight. After a valiant effort on my part, he gained on me, then easily slammed my hand down into my pack that had acted as our table. In fact, he twisted my arm with enough force that I fell, and my whole body plummeted down the gentle slope, my face narrowly missing a boulder.

*Ugh, how embarrassing, and phew, that was close.* I silently thanked God that a concussion wasn't on the day's agenda, but I grimaced as my face scraped the rocky trail. Owww. *Thanks, Marshall.* Incredulous and shocked to find myself sprawled on the ground, I barely processed what had just happened. So much for trying to win.

"Marlee! Are you okay?" Four voices shouted. I glared back. Horrified at what he caused, Marshall was the first to my side to help me up, but I jerked my arm away from him. Ellie unzipped the first aid kit as she hurried down, and Lydie and Sawyer were right behind Marshall. Even Thad seemed concerned.

"I'm fine," I said, but I felt like crying. My cheek was burning from the abrasion, and everyone just watched me tumble over my backpack. How mortifying! Marshall looked ready to punch himself by now. Even though I was mad, I didn't want him to feel too guilty, since I knew that since last summer he had been trying to not be so critical of himself. I just hoped nobody would bring up a similar incident from last summer when he pushed his brother, who fell because of Marshall's teasing shove. I had no doubt that Marsh – our affectionate nickname for Marshall – remembered it vividly, but a public reminder of that mistake was the last thing he needed to help him respect himself. I bit back my snarky thoughts.

"Dude, when you're trying to snag a chick, ya' need to be a little more gentle." Thad laughed. "Not many girls like getting thrown into rocks." I knew Thad was trying to lighten the situation, but I didn't like the way *he* called me a *chick*, and I suddenly felt very defensive for Marsh. How could Thad make jokes like he's one of us? Besides, only last summer Marshall and I had a long talk about how important it is to treat guys respectfully. My anger shifted from Marshall for throwing me down to Thad for humiliating Marshall.

He needed support, so I said, "Good thing for Marshall, I consider this to be just another training session. One of these days I'll take him down." I gave Marshall a *half*-teasing smile. I was still a little mad at him.

Thad chuckled and Marshall gave me a shy, but appreciative, smile. I guess it is partly true, even if I didn't say that just to encourage him. I've always enjoyed wrestling with Dad, and I don't feel uncomfortable when Sawyer and Marshall elbow me and lightly bump my shoulder when we're joking. Roughhousing play can be fun, at least until someone gets hurt. This horseplay was a bit rough for me though, and Ellie told me to sit down while she reached for a peroxide wipe.

By the time Ellie cleaned my left cheek and applied antibacterial cream, I felt less like crying. It's not really my fault that I fell, and it could have been much worse. I could be facing a concussion or a bashed skull if my head had hit the boulder. But part of me still felt like crying with so many eyes on me and my cheek burning. Marshall sulked to the back of the group looking disgusted with the situation. Sawyer urged Ellie to carefully apply zinc oxide to the scrape so the flesh wouldn't sunburn. As she gently rubbed it in, I realized that the abrasion extended from my cheekbone to my jawbone. *How attractive.*

Would I have a scar right on my face? I *try* not to worry too much about my appearance, but let's be honest, I do worry about how I look. My parents have always encouraged us to focus on improving our inner beauty. But suddenly I wondered if I'd still be pretty, at least in Dad's eyes, with a scar right across my face. *That's ridiculous*, my conscience argued. My friend Braelynn's mom has a large birthmark on her face, and most of the time I don't even notice the oddly colored flesh. I guess I look past it. And she's the perfect example of having such an inner beauty that it radiates out and surpasses physical flaws. *I guess I need to work on my inner beauty. Get my character in tip-top shape so my facial wound will be overlooked. And besides, if I take care of it the scar might fade. A girl can hope.*

As if reading my mind, Sawyer lightly said, "Well, Marlee, you know what they say, 'Scars are tattoos with better stories.'" I smiled at his attempt to make me feel better.

"Too bad she doesn't have a good story for that one." Marshall sounded glum.

"Are you kidding?" Lydie joked, "Marlee can tell people that she earned her scar when she got into a wrestling match with a wild mountain man in the backcountry!"

Lydie's joke made us all chuckle, as usual, although Marsh still looked blue.

"Careful what you wish for," Thad suddenly said.

We all looked at him with surprise, and I must admit I was slightly alarmed. He shrugged and said, "Not everyone in the backcountry is good. Once in a while a person can meet up with a bad group."

*What is he talking about?* Backpackers are generally harmless people. Usually we're stinky, and some hikers are a bit eccentric, but not *dangerous*. I studied Thad's face, trying to make sense of his last statement. Did he think *we're* a bad group? Or was he making some unusual joke? Sneaking a peek toward Sawyer, I saw that he too was staring at Thad, no doubt having the same thoughts as me. I was struck with a terrifying thought that shocked my mind like a bolt of lightning: could Thad be a threat to us?

# CHAPTER 4

After an awkwardly silent moment, Ellie returned her first aid kit to her pack and skillfully put it on her back. The rest of us quietly followed suit, but glancing at the faces of my group, it seemed that Sawyer and I were the only ones still pondering Thad's unexpected comment.

The final two miles of the day's hike went smoothly, although we were very thirsty toward the end since we shared so much of our water with Thad. I'd been absorbed in troubling thoughts about what Thad had said, and I suddenly realized that this was the quietest our group of five had ever been. Usually we talked for most of the hike, and sometimes Lydie would even sing little ditties for us, usually oldies songs that make everyone feel happy. Even our main introvert, Marshall, often contributes to the conversations. But as I watched the rocky ridgeline growing taller to the north, I noticed that the only voices I'd heard this evening belonged to Ellie and Thad.

Pushing my thoughts of concern aside, I focused on their conversation. Maybe listening in would show me a different side of Thad and prove that there was no hidden meaning when he said, *"Not everyone in the backcountry is good. Once in a while a person can meet up with a bad group."* Those words had been haunting me. Trying to think realistically, I told myself that Thad probably said those words without a second thought. Surely I was overthinking the whole situation.

"So, come on, Ellie, tell me your favorite part of backpacking. What draws you to the beauty of the trails?" Thad said in a suave voice. I squirmed inwardly.

Sawyer's shoulders stiffened, and he pretended to be highly interested in the rock structure to our left. I really didn't think Ellie meant to flirt with Thad, but her sweet, cheery response about enjoying the outdoors and the challenge and the simplicity of life on the trail could definitely seem flirty to Thad. The way he hung on her every word made me think he was desperate for a girlfriend – or just weird. I wondered if Ellie was enjoying having Thad in our group. She giggled as he made a corny joke, and for the first time in a long time I felt great sympathy for Sawyer because of Ellie. I used to always feel bad for him when Ellie would fly off the handle and yell at him, but this was totally different. They were really close these days, and Ellie was acting chummy with a creepy stranger, and pretty much ignoring Sawyer.

*What was Sawyer thinking?* For the past year, he and Ellie have talked on the phone regularly. And a few times when Sawyer was home on breaks, the Miles boys drove five hours to meet us girls to plan this summer's trips. Each time they visited, Ellie dressed up just a bit, presumably for Sawyer since she's usually pretty casual at home. I mean, she's immaculately clean when we have the luxury of a shower, but her everyday clothes consist of comfy jeans and cute sweaters. But when Sawyer came over, she always wore one of her favorite tunics over black leggings and her tall boots that she saved her money for ages to buy. They always sat next to each other at the table as we studied maps, and they exchanged the sweetest smiles. I wouldn't have been as worried if Sawyer had said what I almost wished he had said earlier: *"Hey, man, I see you're digging my best friend Ellie, and, well, you need to stop, because I've secretly had my eyes on her for the last half-decade and I have plans to date her."*

Marshall had privately told me that the only reason Sawyer hasn't asked her on a real I'm-actually-thinking-of-marrying-you-someday kind of date yet was because he wants to complete his mountaineering guide requirements first, so he can treat dating Ellie like a real, meaningful relationship. Until then, he's sticking to group dates and an occasional, "Hey El, want to go have ice cream with me?" According to Marsh, Sawyer thinks that if he starts dating Ellie seriously before he has a full-time, "grown-up" job, it would seem like he wasn't mature enough to pursue her. I was impressed when Marshall told me that, and I figured that "pursue" meant to consider marriage seriously. The whole dating and marriage topic kind of weirds me out, but I guess the future is on its way, like it or not. And based on Ellie and Sawyer's dramatic changes, I figure that I'll warm up to the idea eventually.

When Marsh and I had that conversation early this spring, I was a bit shocked to consider that Sawyer could actually be thinking of Ellie as his potential wife. But I'd been rooting for them to admit they liked each other for years. And why should people date – for real, not just as friends hanging out – if they're not considering marriage? And they are eighteen now, almost nineteen. I even had the thought that they were legally old enough to marry, but I laughed to myself, realizing they both had some growing up to do before they would take that step.

Sawyer must have felt horribly frustrated to see Ellie, *his* Ellie, chatting happily with Thad while he was flirting with her. *Our Ellie. Mine and Lydie's.* I snapped out of my thoughts as Thad pointed down an unmaintained game trail. He explained that it was the best way to get to the creek to filter water. Carefully picking our path down the rocky bank of the sparkling stream, I was reminded again of the refreshing taste and feel of mountain water. We each found a spot to gather water, and at this location we were all pretty close together. I plopped onto a smooth rock and my legs instantly appreciated the break.

Digging out my pump-style filter and my three empty one-liter bottles from my pack, I tossed the intake line into a shallow pool behind some rocks just before a tiny waterfall and started pumping. I have always loved pumping water. I find it calming. It gives me a chance to look and listen and simply enjoy the pure scenery while my legs rest.

Just when my first liter was full, Thad said, in his fearful, suspicious tone that he used when he questioned us about our plan, "Well, kids, I appreciate your help. I reckon you've done all you can to help me, and I'll remember your kindness." He shot a smile at Ellie and continued his script. "I feel confident that I can make it from here. We're very close to where I'll camp tonight, but I suggest you continue another mile before stopping to camp." *It hasn't been seven miles,* I thought, confused. *I think he lied to us. Or he's lying now. But why?*

Thad didn't politely suggest that we continue another mile, but rather gave the vibe that he specifically didn't want us to camp in the designated campsite. It made me feel weird, so I looked at our guide to gauge his response.

Sawyer quizzically tilted his head at Thad. "Dude, we've been hiking all day and it's almost sunset now. We're younger than you, and we aren't familiar with these trails. Setting out to go another mile will take at least an hour, and we're not up to that, especially since we'll still be pumping water for at least ten or fifteen more minutes." His voice sounded patient, but I could see in his face that he was more than a little irked at Thad.

Although Sawyer would never say it out loud, we had to remember that Lydie, though strong, is twelve, and, no offense to her, she is just not as strong as the rest of us. She works very hard to keep up, and it takes a lot out of her. We all know that she needs eleven hours of sleep while she's backpacking, and her appetite easily competes with Marshall's. I was not complaining about having Lydie along, by any means. And like Lydie, I was more than ready for supper and a good night's rest. Sitting in the hot sun while Thad recovered this afternoon drained us of our energy. We knew our bodies' needs and limits, and Sawyer was assertively standing up for all of us, not just Lydie.

Thad faced Sawyer, and met his level of assertion. "Well, from what I can tell so far, Sawyer, you are a good hiker leading a good group. I'll camp at this next site, and you all need to go on to the following site. You're strong and up to the challenge. The trail's easy and if you start now you'll make it before the sun goes down. The trail crosses the creek just twenty feet upstream, so you're basically on the path anyway." He pointed across the water at a trail marker tied to a large fir tree. "There's your trail. Follow it down into a valley, hike along the meadow of flowers, cross another creek, and you'll come right to the campsite."

*Excuse me?* I thought angrily. *We helped you stay alive and now you want us to hike an extra mile at dusk? Why don't YOU go ahead? We gave you our water and sat with you in the sun and you want to steal our campsite? What is your deal, Thad?* And suddenly, I was again haunted by the reminder of his earlier statement, *"Not everyone in the backcountry is good. Once in a while a person can meet up with a bad group."* Was it possible that Thad knew of trouble near the campsite and wanted to protect us? But if there was impending trouble, why would he stay there? Or, returning to the nagging wonder at the back of my mind, what if Thad was dangerous?

Half of my brain rapidly processed the situation, weighing our options. The other half rapidly prayed for guidance for us, especially for Sawyer. I could only imagine the pressure he felt to make the right decision. Just as I felt ready to melt down into an angry, tired, and scared sob, Sawyer cleared his throat. "All right, Thad, if you're sure you're better and want to camp alone, we'll press on."

"Great, thanks." Thad was obviously relieved as he shook Sawyer's hand. He nodded his appreciation to the rest of us, and then he gave another arrogant, flirty smile to Ellie before admitting that our group was a real help to him. That was true! I didn't know how long Thad would have lasted before dying. Or maybe he wouldn't have died from heat exhaustion. I really didn't know, but I was curious, so I decided to ask Sawyer later. Either way, Thad wouldn't be here now if it hadn't been for us helping him. Without any more thanks or good-byes, or even filling a second bottle, Thad dashed back up the game trail and out of sight. Weirdo.

For a moment, we all just looked at each other. "Won't he need more water than that?" Lydie asked. Sawyer put his finger to his lips, telling her to be quiet. He waved his hand for us to come closer, and I hoped he had an explanation for Thad's hasty departure and clear separation from our group. I could tell that Ellie desperately wanted to say something, but she bit her tongue and waited for Sawyer to talk before taking her turn. Looking up the trail once again, Sawyer whispered, "I'm so sorry to make us keep going, but something about Thad makes me think we need to get away from him."

"Come on, bro," Marshall jokingly interrupted, "you're just jealous of Thad and want to get Ellie away from him." I glanced sideways at

Ellie to see her eyebrows pop up in surprise and then at Sawyer to see him glare at Marshall.

"That too," Sawyer slowly admitted, his gaze softening. *Maybe Acadia isn't his news.* I sure hoped not. "But some of the stuff he said doesn't add up. And frankly, since he made it very clear that he doesn't want us anywhere near him, I think we need to take the hint and get away from him. Maybe there's a reason he wants plenty of space." Sawyer slowly shook his head as if still thinking about Thad's words.

I eagerly nodded. "I agree with Sawyer. I know we're all tired and hungry, but there's something untrustworthy about that guy. Like for instance, he said he had seven miles to go and it's only been two, and now he wants to camp here. Of course, he had heat exhaustion, so it's possible he wasn't thinking straight, but I still say we push on. I'm starting to wonder if he ever thinks straight. Let's just get away from him." I glanced toward Lydie and tried to get a rating on her energy. She looked tired, but resigned to the plan of going an extra mile, and I determined that she would be all right.

Ellie nodded, but a moment later started to say, "But, what if..." she trailed off.

"Go ahead, Ellie. What is it?" Sawyer encouraged.

"Maybe this is far-fetched," Ellie slowly said, as if she was afraid to say it, "but what if there's something wrong at the next campsite where Thad sent us? I mean, he doesn't want us to be near him, but why? Do you think it's a coincidence that he said that not everyone you meet in the backcountry is good? What if he's planning some crime against us, and we'll hike right into it by following his instructions?"

Sawyer, Lydie, and I nodded thoughtfully, but Marshall's eyebrows crinkled in disagreement. "Good point, but I think it's more likely that he's afraid of us, so he'll feel better if he knows we're out of his space. He seemed paranoid when he was asking every detail of our itinerary. Like he thought we were out to get him. And how could he be planning evil against us when he was half-dead only a few hours ago?" Again, we all nodded thoughtfully, considering the unusual situation. Was it paranoia or planned crime? If he really was a criminal, he could have accomplices, and they could still be able to do whatever it was even if Thad was sick. He looked nervous – was it fear of us hurting him, or of us spoiling his criminal plans?

"Not trying to change the subject," Lydie said, "but should we return this map that fell out of his pack?"

"Huh?" Sawyer asked.

"When he pulled his water filter out of his pack, I noticed this small map fall out. He left in such a hurry that I forgot to mention it," Lydie said.

Sawyer and Marsh walked over to look at the map. "The guy wasn't making it up when he said he likes cartography. This looks like a home-drawn map he's working on. It looks like this area," he said, pointing out a few features to Marshall. "See this steep increase in elevation? That looks like the ridge to the north," Sawyer explained to his brother, referring to the rocky ridge along the left side of the trail adjacent to where we had recently been. "If I'd worked on this, I would definitely want it back," Sawyer said. "Or, we could leave it here, since he'll probably be back for more water in the morning and find it. But then again, it's paper and won't survive a night of dew and breezes." Sawyer studied each of our faces, silently asking our opinions.

"Let's go together to return it to Thad," I heard myself suggest. *Seriously?* "Hopefully returning it will turn over a new leaf, and we'll all be reassured that the other isn't a threat. It could be that he's just super tired and still regaining strength from his close call this afternoon, but he's embarrassed for us to see him get weak and crash, so he doesn't want to camp with us."

Everyone agreed with my idea, and with Sawyer still studying the homemade map, we loaded up our packs.

Before we headed up the trail, Sawyer held up a hand. "Hang on. We're not taking the trail to Thad's site. We're going off trail, leaving no trace, and hiking quietly."

Ellie opened her mouth to protest, but Sawyer simply shook his head. "There's something about that guy. If he's still on the trail, I don't want to bump into him like this, carrying his property." I figured that no real harm would come from us going slightly off trail just once. After all, the only reason we were going off trail was to escape danger, and our parents had explicitly warned us not to risk danger. Dad has always said that a slight change in plans was better than an impulsive and unnecessary risk. In about two minutes, we could see through the trees that we were approaching a clearing. Before we stepped into the campsite, we heard Thad's voice in a hushed, urgent tone. In the dusk, I couldn't see him, but his voice sounded like we were very close.

"About time you answered," Thad's voice grumbled. "I pay the bill for these satellite phones; the least you could do is use yours and *help* me." We glanced at each other, motionless, as Thad's voice continued. "Yeah, well I'm in a tough spot here. I have five goodie two-shoes on my case and I need backup to get rid of them." A pause. "Yes, *you*. Listen, I'm at my favorite campsite by the creek, close to where I'm sure Grandpa's cache is. I sent the good Samaritans onto Meadowlark Campsite, but I need to start digging just after sunset – so in like half an hour – if I'm going to find Grandpa's treasure and finish before sunrise. I need you to get rid of these kids." Another pause. "I already *told* you. Five of them. They're decent hikers, so they'll be at Meadowlark within the hour." A longer pause. "Figure it out, Dude. Act like a ranger and insist on escorting them out for something, a fire in the area or something. Something serious enough that they'll believe you. But listen, do not get violent with these kids. We can't get in trouble. It'll only draw more attention to Grandpa's hidden treasure. And if I ever meet that stupid SMiles on the Trail blogger I'm going to give him the old one-two punch. That blog post about rumors of buried treasures in the backcountry had like three hundred views." *Oh, that's bad.* I was so glad that Sawyer didn't tell Thad his last name.

A moment of eerie quiet, and then we heard, "I'm positive. One hundred percent. Grandpa and I studied the map perfectly, and we know it's here. I can feel it. I'm getting it this time, and I just changed my mind about quitting at sunrise. I'll take as much time as needed, even if it takes me the next twenty-four hours. If I'm still looking tomorrow at this time, I'll sleep and you'll guard before I start again."

Mouths open, we five exchanged flabbergasted looks. Then Thad added, "Oh yeah, the girls are cute. Especially the oldest. She's smoking. Man, I could have some real fun with her if she wasn't such a goody-goody. But I can see a mile away that her halo is on too tight to do anything with her." Quiet. "My mind's always in the gutter. Of *course* I flirted with her, partly for fun, partly to tick off their leader, Sawyer. Thought if I made a move on her, he'd get mad and make his group ditch me." Quiet. "Nah. They're all too perfect."

Ellie quietly gasped and stepped back really nervously, bumping into Sawyer, who protectively put a hand on her elbow. I think we girls were a bit appalled to hear what Thad said about Ellie. I realized that she, and even me and Lydie, shouldn't be anywhere near him. He might not actually be a threat, but he certainly couldn't be trusted. Sawyer did not look very surprised, although even in the growing dark I could see he had a thoroughly disgusted look.

"Back to business. A real ranger wouldn't flirt on duty, so don't even look at the oldest girl or you'll wreck this whole plan. Ignore the middle one too, she's probably sixteen or seventeen and cute enough to distract you. Listen, you need to come at them from the south on Wild Berry Trail, and fast. Get them out of here. Hike them through the night." Thad listened for a moment. "Yeah, if it was as serious as a wildfire or poachers a ranger would hike them out at night. Get going! Are you even standing up yet? *Hel-lo?*"

"Oh no," Thad said with a note of panic. "Dude, *tell me* you're playing a mean prank. Where's my map? No! I had it hidden with my water filter! It must've fallen out at the creek. How could I have let that happen?" He grunted. "*Not* a good start to the biggest night of my life. I'm going to the creek, then returning to my site. You come from the south on Wild Berry Trail to Meadowlark Campsite and get rid of my annoying tagalongs. They seem harmless, but nobody, and I mean nobody, can know about Grandpa's treasure." Pause. "Good. Thanks, man."

I was literally shaking from the conversation we had just heard. And then it occurred to me that Thad would take the trail he previously used to get to the creek. Sawyer was exactly right that we should have gone off trail! *Thank you, God, for putting that thought in his mind!*

"I can't believe this is happening," Marshall said flatly, as if almost in shock.

"What should we do?" Lydie loudly whispered to Sawyer, her eyes widening to a huge, worried size and her voice trembling. Even though she was pretty mature for her age, she was still the youngest child. We older kids, especially Ellie and, during our summer trips, Sawyer, had carried the brunt of the problem-solving. Lydie was used to having someone there for her, and had that trust of a younger sibling. Just like I trust Ellie. Lydie needed reassurance.

Ellie seemed to be thinking the same thing as she took Lydie's hand and stroked her hair with her other hand, looking protective, but still as nervous as any of the rest of us. She glanced at me with concern too, but seemed to be deciding that I didn't need her as much anymore. Like she thought that I would be okay. *But I do need you, Ellie! What could I ever do without you?* For the first time, I thought of the responsibility to look out for Lydie that would fall on my shoulders if Ellie ever moved away. I wanted someone there for me too. Was that selfish? I hoped not, but no way could I fill Ellie's shoes as the oldest. I wondered if Ellie ever thought about what would happen if she moved away. Maybe she didn't want to let me take care of myself any more than I wanted to. But there wasn't time to worry about that with a treasure hunter's sidekick after us. And anyway, I decided to just focus on the knowledge that God would always be there for me. It was a good thought for all of us!

Sawyer's eyes surveyed the area, thinking rapidly. Speaking slowly and deliberately, he said, "We'll pray silently as we go. We'll go as quickly and quietly as we can and won't turn on our headlamps until we're *at least* two miles away from Thad."

"Which way do we go?" Ellie butted in.

Sawyer silently looked north to the tall, rocky ridge behind us, a sobered look on his face. Ellie slowly shook her head. "How Sawyer? How can we climb that with our packs on? There has to be another way."

Sawyer shook his head. "Thad's sidekick is coming from the south. We can't go south. And we don't want to be anywhere near Thad's dig site. If we continue our path from today, going northeast on the same trail, that guy will overtake us as soon as Wild Berry Trail meets ours, since he'll have energy and Thad told him to hurry. We've been hiking all day and haven't had a meal since breakfast. And there are five of us. Sounds like his sidekick has been laying low waiting for instructions. He's probably already running this way. He'll be scouring the whole area around Thad's site and the Meadowlark Campsite for us. They won't expect that we'll climb the ridge. It's our only hope."

We let Sawyer's plan settle in our minds. I was already nervous. We've done some rock climbing, but I'm not great. Especially with a heavy pack. And at the end of a long day. And in the dark. And in hiking boots rather than climbing shoes, or at the very least, tennis shoes. I was starting to get very scared of this situation, but Sawyer interrupted my fearful thoughts.

"Marlee, as fast as you can, take a picture of this map and then I'll put it in Thad's campsite. He'll probably be back in just a few minutes. We need to start running."

Absentmindedly, I grabbed my camera from the top of my pack, adjusted the settings for the dark, and snapped a few pictures of Thad's homemade map before I got one shot that showed it accurately.

"Good, thanks. You all get a start. Run. I'll catch up in a moment. Watch your steps like a hawk. We can't afford to have anyone fall now. Run fast and run carefully. Ellie, you lead the way to the ridge."

"You shouldn't be alone," Ellie quickly protested. She was right. It was a cardinal rule of hiking.

Sawyer sighed, as if he had thought of it but decided he'd be faster alone. Nodding, he replied, "Well, I don't want the girls to be without a guy. Ellie or Marlee, who can sprint faster?" Sawyer asked. I pointed at Ellie and stepped closer to Lydie and Marshall. "Marsh, you're the leader," Sawyer said.

Marshall looked nearly panicked as he stepped to the lead position, so I elbowed him and gave an encouraging nod. He weakly smiled his thanks. Still shaking, I started to run behind Marshall, and I made sure I could hear Lydie behind me. I'd need to glance back often to make sure we didn't lose her. My habit of rapidly praying to God kicked in, and, overwhelmed with the situation, a tear trickled down my cheek as my lungs and legs screamed for a rest. But I kept running – away from the danger, and toward the hope provided by the tall ridge.

# CHAPTER 5

In the background, I heard shouting. Or at least it sounded like a voice yelling. I looked over my shoulder, and there was Lydie running with all her heart. This was hard for all of us, but I knew it was even harder for her. She looked almost ready to collapse. I felt pressure on my face as my pulse throbbed beneath the cut. Marshall was so fast, and my throat burned from breathing so hard and trying to keep him in sight as he ducked under branches, hopped over bushes, and weaved between rocks and trees. I checked on Lydie again, and I was glad she had had some rest time earlier when we found Thad, even if it was hot sitting there in the sun. After another long minute of fighting the enormous temptation to stop, I realized Sawyer and Ellie were close behind. I heard their breathing and their steps. When I glanced back again, they were stopped, and it looked like Sawyer was taking Lydie's pack. That would help her considerably, and likely wouldn't impact Sawyer very much. He trains so hard that carrying Lydie's small pack on his front wouldn't slow him down enough to matter.

Squinting in the dark, I kept running toward Marshall's shadow, and just when I felt like I couldn't continue, I crashed right into Marshall. "Oof!" Air rushed out of my lungs as we collided and fell on the ground. "Sorry," I whispered between desperate breaths. We scrambled to stand again, still gasping.

Marshall gave me a serious look in the dark and then pointed up. I followed the direction of his arm, and in the dim light between twilight and true darkness I could see the rocky ridge towering above us. As my panting slowed, I wondered how we could possibly climb it in the dark, in a hurry.

Sawyer, Ellie and Lydie reached us a moment later, and Lydie looked every bit as drained as I felt. But something else caught my attention. Sawyer and Ellie looked panicked. "What's wrong?" I asked between fast breaths.

"We need to get over this quickly. I wish we had gear and time for one of us to lead climb it and set a top rope anchor for the rest of us. I didn't want to carry all the extra weight of climbing gear, since we weren't planning on any rock climbing, and anyway, Thad caught us returning the map, and now he's convinced we're going to steal his treasure," Sawyer quickly and quietly explained. My eyes widened as Sawyer relayed this information. I *hadn't* imagined the yelling. It was Thad – shouting at Sawyer and Ellie.

"He wouldn't listen when we insisted that we didn't want his map or treasure, and he said he's going to catch us. So we ran. He was stuffing some tools in his pack, but he's probably not far behind us now! Let's hurry." Ellie's voice was shaky.

Lydie leaned into Ellie. "What should we do?" Lydie asked Sawyer, looking at him like a little girl looks at a beloved uncle. I admired her resilience and ability to trust Sawyer as our guide. In contrast, I was starting to wonder why I agreed to have Sawyer lead us again after last summer's event. First an avalanche – now *this*.

Sawyer didn't hesitate to keep directing us though. "Quick! We have to be as quiet as possible. I wish we could stick together, but I really think we have to split up. Ellie and I will go with Lydie. Marshall, you and Marlee stay together. Leave no trace, make no noise. Find a spot to get over this ridge safely, and *go!* We'll find each other on the other side of it." Sawyer gestured for us all to put a hand in the middle of a circle. As serious as I've ever seen him, he whispered in a barely audible voice, "Godspeed."

Numbly, we bumped fists and departed. With one long look at my sisters, I fought tears as they turned and followed Sawyer along the ridge. I felt like time stood still as I listened to their boots scuffing along the ground, leaving me with Marshall, wondering when I'd see them again. I felt my terrified heart pounding, echoing through my whole body. I tried to pray, but my mind had gone blank and I couldn't form coherent thoughts. *Just please help, God.* Finally, I noticed Marshall urgently grabbing my arm and tugging me toward the ridge wall. "*Mar*-lee!" he whispered. Evidently he had taken off and then noticed I wasn't with him. Good thing he noticed, because I was hardly aware.

I couldn't see my sisters and Sawyer anymore, and I began to wonder if I should've spoken up when Sawyer suggested we split up. Suddenly I felt angry for not thinking, and part of me wanted to turn and run toward Sawyer and my sisters. *No, that wouldn't be wise,* my rational side argued. Five people would make much more noise and be harder to hide than two or three. Smacking my shin into a fallen branch, I was forced out of my thoughts and again became aware of Marshall's presence. He was a few paces ahead of me as we reached the base of the ridge wall. Up close it looked even taller than from afar. He silently gestured his hand up and down the length of the wall, indicating that we needed to scout out a low spot to scramble up the rocky wall.

At first glance, it looked like the lowest spots were still twenty feet above our heads. I tried not to panic as I considered free solo climbing with a heavy pack. *Take that, Acadia.* But I sure felt like panicking! Just when I nearly burst into tears, Marshall turned toward me with a hopeful look on his usually-serious face. I jogged to him and followed his gaze.

About hip-high stuck a root of some kind of tree. It looked strong enough to support us, and if we fell from it, we wouldn't be far off the ground.  From there, it looked like with a stretch we'd be able to reach a reliable "jug," as rock climbers would say. Just so long as the rock wasn't loose, we should be able to work our way up the wall at an angle and, hopefully, make it to the other side before Thad found the same spot. Thad. My heart raced again as he returned to my thoughts. We were being chased. Chased by an angry person who thought we were in the wrong.

My hands felt shaky, but Marshall's quiet yet confident voice forced me to focus on the task at hand. "Come on, Marlee. Normally I'd push past you to prove I'm a better climber, but this time I'll be a gentleman and let you go first. That way you won't be alone down here, and I can spot you until you're shoulder-high in case you slip. Then you'll be on your own, but I'm sure you'll do fine. Looks like the hardest part is the start, and overall the route doesn't look harder than a 5.7 or 5.8." I knew he was referring to the Yosemite Decimal System, the American rating scale for rock climbing. An easy climb would be a 5.5, and 5.15 would be one of the world's hardest climbs. *Even exhausted, I should be able to climb a 5.7 or 5.8.* I longed for a harness and rope, but since that wasn't an option, I wouldn't let my mind entertain the thought of safety gear.

Instead, I breathed a short prayer and just before I stepped forward, Marshall caught my eye. "Come on, Marlee. Let's see you send this. Don't deck out!" He whispered with uncharacteristic arrogance, almost acting like a "rock jock," but I did appreciate his pep talk. *But when did he start using climber jargon?* As if reading my puzzled thoughts, he grinned and said, "I heard Sawyer say that once and have always wanted to say it too."

I loosened my shoulder straps a wee bit, snugged up the load stabilizing straps and stretched the toe of my right boot all the way up to hip-height. I've never been super flexible, not like a gymnast, but this was one of those many moments when I was extra thankful to be a girl and possess at least some level of oh-so-necessary flexibility.

"Spotter ready?" I instinctively whispered the safety call.

"Spotter ready. Climb on," Marshall responded.

Trusting him I whispered, "Climbing," and kept my eyes forward. He put his hand on my pack to help stabilize me if I needed it. Hooking my toe on the root, I leaned my upper body forward and, with full contact between my hands and the rock, I stepped up. I carefully and fairly skillfully moved my hands to feel for any crack or pocket or crimp to help me balance until I could grab the jug-handle rock. I wobbled for a second before my left hand located a small undercling, which I clutched onto with all my strength. Feeling more confident with one hand balanced, I stretched up with my right hand and reached the jug.

Giving it a little shove, I checked its stability and was relieved to find it solid. Had it wobbled, it wouldn't have been safe to use as a hold. For double measure, I knocked my knuckles on it. It didn't sound hollow, which was also a well-placed miracle. I glanced down to Marshall and gave him a nod, letting him know that the jug seemed like a good hold for us to use. He let go of my pack.

My hands were steadier, but I knew it was best to climb with leg muscles, rather than upper body strength since the lower body is so much stronger. I began looking for anything suitable that my feet could reach. It was getting dark enough that I had to strain my eyes for a moment before I could identify my next foothold. Lifting my left foot up to knee-height, my toe easily fit on a small ledge, and I nervously stepped up. "Nice," I heard Marshall murmur. "You're past spotting height now, Marlee, but it also looks like you're past the hardest part. Keep digging, and once you top out, I'll send. Don't get Elvis leg or crux out." *What did he just say?* If not for the seriousness of the situation, I would've laughed at his use of climber lingo. I *think* he essentially said "don't fall," but apparently Sawyer had heard lots of the unique language at the climbing gym and shared it with Marshall, who was obviously thrilled to have a chance to use it.

Even though it sounded a little silly coming from the usual-ly-not-so-confident Marshall, I had to admit that it helped me get in the climbing state of mind. I decided that for the rest of the ascent, I'd stoke myself up with whatever Marshall had said with his rock-jock talk about cruxing out and Elvis leg. I felt unqualified to use climber jargon, but I kept thinking if I really thought of myself as a skilled climber, it would help me through this. Sawyer had left a climbing magazine at our house a few months ago, so I was vaguely familiar with some of the terms. If only I had more skill! *Please, God. We really need help.*

Marshall was right about my being past the difficult part. I was pretty much walking up a steeply sloped set of stairs, using my hands only for balance. I took the opportunity to look down and could barely see Marshall's outline in the dark. *Whoa. Were those TREES below me?! Steady, girl! Not a good time to worry about the ground.*

Looking ahead again, I saw that I was mostly on top of the ridge now, so I quietly called down to Marshall that he could begin climbing.

He started up the same route I took, and I wrung my hands together and tried to steady my nerves. I made it safely up the free solo climb. My first – and hopefully only – free solo. Mom and Dad would flip out. Even the most trained climbers have accidents free soloing. It's a do or die sport. I had to sit down for a second, but felt so rattled that I stood and took a few more steps up the wall, which continued to climb in elevation toward a nearby peak. I surveyed the terrain up there. It was what Dad would call talus, meaning medium to large-sized rocks or boulders all wedged together. Of course we'd be on the lookout for loose rocks, but since it was talus, the rocks would mostly be steady. The width of the wall looked like it varied from one foot to six feet, so there would be no shoving each other *at all*. That's when it occurred to me that we'd have to find a safe route down the other side. *Okay, make that one out of hopefully only two free solos.* Then I heard Marshall's boots on the rocks, telling me he made it too. Just as I was turning to give him a little high-five, we heard Thad. "I know you're here, kids! If you have half a mind, you'll hike as far away from me as you can and as fast as you can go! Get out of my territory, all of you!"

# CHAPTER 6

I froze, but Marshall thought quickly enough to duck down, spreading his body on the rocks. He was close enough to gently tug my ankle, and he hissed, "Get *down*!" Going slowly, hoping not to attract attention, I began to squat down, gradually wriggling to my stomach, and wishing I could be invisible. I couldn't see Thad, or even the ground, but where we were on the ridge was still in the dusk light, so if he was looking up, he'd be able to see us. Crouching down further, my toe bumped a pebble which took off down the wall. Marshall grabbed for it, but it was out of his reach as it accelerated in speed and noise. *Dear God, please don't let Thad notice!* I desperately prayed. But when even tiny rocks fall like that, they bounce and become very noticeable by the time they reach the ground. I was so mad at myself for kicking down a pebble.

Sure enough, Thad noticed the flying stone and correctly assumed that it fell because of our scrambling. Wanting to melt into the rock completely, I held my breath as Thad shouted some more at us. "You *are* up there! I knew it! So you're decent climbers! But you're not sneaky enough! Listen, don't you dare come within a mile of my Grandpa's cache! Get outta here *now!*"

*What do we do? If we get up and leave, he'll know for sure where we are. But if we stay, there's a possibility he'll think we're not here and that the rock just happened to fall. But if he sees us, and sees that we don't move, he'll keep thinking we're after his treasure. What did Sawyer write in his blog post anyway?* Before we could do anything, we heard Thad turn and head back toward "his territory." Marshall was right to duck down and hide on the rock.

I tried to suppress my breathing, but my heart was thumping so hard I figured Marshall and maybe even Thad could hear it. We didn't hear Thad for a moment, and that's when Marshall whispered, "We're going to stay absolutely silent for about three minutes, and if he's still gone, we'll leave then." I nodded and focused on slowing my breath. My hands were shaking, and if I had been standing, I'm certain my knees would have been knocking. *And I just free soloed!* I thanked God fervently for protecting us during the climb and for getting Thad to leave.

I was stunned with our crisis. How had we hiked into such danger? And after saving Thad's life! *We dropped everything to help him, and now he's acting like we want to find his hidden treasure?* I felt disgusted that we bothered to help him. *What a horrible person. Wait, Marlee. That's not right. Even though he's ridiculously defensive of whatever he's searching for, he's still a person. We would've been the horrible ones if we had hiked past and not offered to help. We can only make ourselves do what we're supposed to, and if he's acting like this, it's his problem. Too bad he's such a problem for us.*

All I could do was pray, and when my blood finally stopped boiling and my heart seemed to be thumping at a quieter level, Marsh shook my ankle and I heard him stand up. He offered me his hand. "You really did do a nice job climbing that, Marlee," he whispered as I slowly stood, careful to not kick more rocks loose.

"Thanks." I smiled as I took his hand. "I guess you rocked it too, but I didn't get to see it." In the dark, I think I saw him smile before he gestured with his hand to walk behind a higher spot on the wall. Too bad we hadn't made it to this concealed location when Thad was looking for us.

When we were hidden from the direction in which Thad stormed off, Marshall whispered, "I say we hike along the top of the ridge, scout out the area, try to see where Thad is, see if we can locate Sawyer, El and Lyd, and try to figure out the best place for us to go from here."

*Has he lost his mind?* "Marsh, it's dark and we've never been here before. We can't use our headlamps since Thad's after us, the others are probably already on their way down *like planned*, and you're suggesting we hike along this narrow, rocky ridge – we're talking *one foot* in some places – at night, with a thirty-foot drop off on either side? We could easily get killed!"

Marshall irritably sighed. He grows weary of communicating with us girls, so I almost regretted contradicting him. "Marlee, please hear me out. I think an aerial view of this whole area would help me orient where we are and where we should go."

Okay, I heard him, but I still disagreed. "Sawyer told us to get over the ridge and meet on the other side. He didn't tell us to *wander* around at the top. We'll meet the others on the bottom, out of Thad's view, study the map, and make the best plan from there," I tried to rationalize.

"Nobody ever believes me," Marshall muttered under his breath. "Why does everything I say automatically have zero-credibility?"

*Because it's a horrible idea!* I could sense Marshall's blood boiling now.

He shook his head. "Fine, you go down and I'll scout around up here. Then I'll come down and find you."

Marshall spun on his heel and started off to the right, up the inclining top of the wall.

"Great," I muttered with disgust. I groaned and followed him. He had a point about seeing the situation from above. But that didn't mean I thought picking our way along the top of a rock wall in the dark was advisable. I shook my head as I carefully picked my steps behind him.

"Oh, so you *are* coming?" Marshall snapped when he noticed me trying to catch up.

I tried to ignore his rudeness, and turned it into a joke by saying, "You're not ever supposed to hike alone. Besides, someone will need to know where your body lands." He shook his head and grunted. *Okay, maybe not the best thing to say, Marlee. Oops.* I sighed, disappointed with myself. We were all hungry. And exhausted. And getting grouchy. And we didn't even know where we'd be camping. Or if we'd camp that night. I sighed again at the thought of hiking through the night.

"Look how this ridge goes all the way to the peak." Marshall pointed ahead.

"Want to attempt the summit tonight?" I teasingly asked in an attempt to lighten the mood. Marshall chuckled and the tension was reduced. I do appreciate how quickly Marshall gets over anger, but our spat from the previous moments reminded me that I needed to tread carefully, especially when we were so exhausted and hungry. We'd walked probably eighty feet atop the ridge when we heard voices and stopped in our tracks. Hoping it was Sawyer, Ellie and Lydie, I smiled at the possibility of reuniting with my sisters and Sawyer. But all we heard was a man's voice, and it sounded distant, and it was coming from the direction of "Thad's territory". I couldn't quite make out what he was saying. Then I recognized Thad's voice speaking in response. Again, the voice was too far away to clearly hear, but at least he wasn't yelling. "So that's where Thad and his sidekick are." Marshall gestured to the right.

I hoped we would descend to the left of the ridge here, but Marshall kept walking. Another hundred or so steps and he suddenly wobbled on a loose rock. I reached out to steady him, but when I grabbed his elbow and the rock teetered back, it threw me off balance too. I fell to my knees with a thud and Marshall stumbled back. His pack cushioned his landing. Thankfully we were in a wider part and neither of us was dangerously close to the edge, but it was really scary for both of us. Close calls might as well be my middle name.

My knees ached from the impact of landing on the rock. In the emotion of the scary close call, my cheeks scrunched and I started to tear up. But when my cheeks scrunched, it made my cut from earlier hurt again, and the pain and memory of my cut made me want to cry more. I didn't want Marshall to see me cry, and I was scared. I'd never been threatened by someone before. Chased out of public land because some paranoid treasure hunter thought we wanted his cache. *Does he even have a right to the treasure?* I tried so hard to hold the tears back, but a sob escaped. Turning my head in the hopes that Marshall wouldn't hear, I let a stubborn tear slip down my stinging cheek. *Ow.*

Marshall crawled over and gently asked, "Do your knees hurt that bad, Marlee?"

I looked away and shrugged, not wanting to be the center of attention. "I'm sorry that you keep getting hurt because of my carelessness," he sincerely said.

"No. I'm just tired and hungry and scared." My voice shook.

Marshall nodded, and to my surprise, he said, "Me too. When we get down let's all have a little gorp." I didn't know Marshall was scared.

I didn't figure that a scared person would suggest we walk atop a rock wall in the dark. I heard him swallow hard. "But at least we're together, and we know that God will never leave us."

I smiled and nodded.

"I'm sorry it took a loose rock and both of us falling to see that it's time for us to get off this wall. Maybe we should have gone down sooner. It's so hard to know what to do sometimes," he stammered. He gave my knee a quick pat and stood, saying that he would find a safe location for us to descend. I nodded, shifting into a seated position, and gently rubbed my bruised knees, glad to be off my feet for the moment.

A few minutes later, Marshall returned with the news that just ahead was a relatively gently sloped spot to go down. I stood, being sure to stay off the loose rock, and we tediously checked each rock before trusting it with our weight. When we got to the edge, Marshall whispered that he thought it was safe to use our headlamps to go down. My eyebrows shot up. I would love the security of light, but could we really risk it with Thad directly across from us?

"Look, Marlee." Marshall pointed behind me toward where we had just come. Looking back, I saw we had already descended at least five feet from the high point of the wall, and as long as we kept our lights pointed down, it was very unlikely that they would be visible to Thad.

Rather than taking off our packs, we took turns reaching into the tops of each other's bags to retrieve our headlamps. Clicking on my lamp shocked my eyes for a moment. I hadn't realized how much I was straining to see in the deepening dark, but with the shine of our lights, we noticed how dark it really was around us. As I carefully descended, following about six feet behind Marshall, I wondered about the rest of our crew. I was hopeful that with our lights on, they would see us and we would easily reunite. Each step I took down brought me comfort that we were more out of Thad's sight and space. I wouldn't mind a few more miles of distance between us, but a tall rock wall was very reassuring – especially in the dark. Few would dare to climb up it in the dark. We were some of the few, though not exactly willingly. For once I wished that we were crazier than Thad and that he wouldn't consider climbing the ridge in the dark. Our parents would be horrified if they knew what we had just done.

Caught in my thoughts, I nearly stepped on Marshall's hand. "Wait!" he said in a hushed, but urgent voice. That's when I noticed he was five feet below me, on the ground, and reaching his hand toward me. "The last step down is really big, Marlee. Let me help you."

I hesitated before accepting his help. Usually I like the challenge of trying to keep up with the boys, and normally I would slip down on my belly without much thought. But thinking of my knees and my cheek and the fact that it was dark made the decision clear. "Be smart and use a spotter," I could almost hear my dad say.

"Should I slide down facing the rock, you think?" I asked Marshall.

"Yeah, I'll spot you." Out of habit, we quickly went through the safety commands before I descended. I could feel that Marshall was holding my pack, ready to support me if at any point I lost control. When I was firmly standing on the ground, we exchanged nods to indicate that I was steady and he let go of my pack.

"We're crazy to do what we just did," I mumbled.

Marshall whispered, "Yeah, but at least this time we didn't plan to do this." I giggled, thinking about last year's sneak side trip that led us into an avalanche. Sometimes I still have scary dreams about roaring snow and struggling to reach air, fighting to find my sisters, and carrying injured Lydie out of the mountains. At those times, the avalanche seems so near in my memory. But right now, in this unbelievable situation of escaping, the avalanche seemed like distant history.

Marshall must have been thinking the same thing, based on the faraway look in his eye. Before either of us said anything, we heard the soft crunching sound made by hiking boots. A rush of fear told me to flee from the sound, but then I heard Lydie's sweet voice loudly whisper, "Hey, we're over here!" Relief surged through me as Lydie and Ellie stepped into the light of my headlamp and wrapped me in hugs. Sawyer clapped Marshall on the shoulder, and they stepped to the side to talk.

"You two were up there for a long time. What took you so long?" Ellie asked. "We were starting to worry."

I shrugged. "Marsh wanted to see the area from above, scout out where to go and where Thad is working."

"You saw him? Weren't you afraid he'd see you?" Lydie asked with wide eyes.

"We didn't see him, but we could hear his voice. Shortly after that, we came down." I didn't think it was a good time to mention how close we came to falling.

The boys joined our circle and Sawyer addressed me. "Marlee, let's look at the picture of the map on your camera. We need to figure out exactly where these guys will be and how to avoid them."

I took off my pack to retrieve the camera, and Sawyer said, "Once we see what area Thad considers his, we need to find a good place to camp tonight. The campsite we planned on is claimed by him," he finished with a grimace.

Handing the camera to Sawyer with the photo of the map displayed, we all were silent as he studied it. Marshall peered over his shoulder. Sawyer's eyebrows furrowed slightly, and I saw Marshall's eyes flash with worry. They exchanged a sideways glance, and then I knew something was wrong. *Like we need more problems.*

"What is it?" Ellie and I simultaneously demanded.

"Hang on," Sawyer said. "Marlee, can you make it zoom in so we can see it better?" I made a quick adjustment and showed him how to scroll across the enlarged photo.

Another minute passed before anyone spoke. I observed the boys' faces as they studied the picture, and finally Marshall sighed, shaking his head. "Tell 'em, bro."

"You girls remember our parents talking about the day trip they plan to take?" Sawyer asked. We all nodded, even though I could only vaguely recall where they planned to go. I remember Mom and Dad talking about a couple of day hikes they planned during our trek, but I guess I was so absorbed with our own plans that I didn't pay close attention to theirs. *Oops. I didn't expect to need to watch out for our parents. It was supposed to be the other way around.* Sawyer held the camera so we all could see the picture of Thad's map. Using his finger as a pointer, he showed us where Thad was working, where we were, and the direction toward where our parents were base camping for the week. Dragging his finger across the map, straight into Thad's territory, he said, "Thad doesn't have the whole trail sketched here, but this is where our parents will be hiking – tomorrow."

# CHAPTER 7

We were all silent for a moment as we let the news sink in. Ellie, who likes to know details before jumping on board, asked, "You're certain that this is where the trail is? And that it's the same trail our parents plan on taking? Why didn't Thad draw the trail on his map if it's in his territory?" Ellie's voice showed disdain as she dramatically emphasized "his territory."

Sawyer seemed to think she had raised a valid question, but he was confident that he had read the clues correctly. Reaching for his own topo map of the area, he compared Thad's homemade map to his professionally-printed map, pointing out a handful of similarities. "He has a little scribble for the trail on both ends of the map. I guess he didn't feel the need to complete it since he knows the area so thoroughly. It'd be like you drawing a map with directions from your house to another location. You wouldn't need to show the part closest to your house since you already know it."

I nodded.

"So what should we do?" Lydie asked.

"I definitely don't want Mom and Dad to have to experience Thad's craziness," Ellie said.

"But if Thad doesn't know they're associated with us, maybe he'll ignore them," Marshall suggested. "He won't want to get into trouble either. And they're adults. He probably wouldn't mess with four adults older than him. He's just bullying us because we're younger." That idea made sense too. We heard him tell his friend not to be violent, so he must not be out to hurt people.

Sawyer shook his head. "Those are valid arguments, but Thad has one thing on his mind, and he seems willing to do whatever it takes to keep everyone else away."

"So can we call them and warn them to change their itinerary?" I asked.

Sawyer exchanged a look with Lydie and Ellie. "Our phones didn't work on the top of the ridge. We tried them quickly, but there was absolutely no service. And if we didn't have service on top of the ridge, there sure won't be any on the ground next to the ridge." That was brilliant of them to turn on their phones and check for service from the high spot!

"And the satellite messenger?" Marshall hurriedly asked.

"Without our phones to write a custom message to then send on the satellite messenger, all we could do is send out an SOS, which would of course alert emergency authorities. But since it's after dark, the rescuers will have to wait until morning to even begin to help us."

"So, suppose we do nothing," Lydie slowly suggested. "Our parents' hike takes them to Thad, they get chewed out by him, they leave and hike somewhere else...right? Do we have to do anything?"

Considering this for a moment before responding, Sawyer finally shook his head. "But you know our moms. They all know our itinerary and that we planned to be in that area. Mom will start to cry and ask Thad what he did to the five kids who hiked through." Marshall nodded, apparently picturing the panic that would cause our parents.

"Then Thad will know that we're associated with them, and as protective of that land as he is, he'll get it in his mind that we are collectively a threat to his grandpa's treasure. No thanks to that SMiles on the Trail blogger," Sawyer shuddered. "That would freak out our parents *and* Thad."

"But shouldn't he be done by morning? By the time our parents even reach this area, Thad and his sidekick should be finished with their treasure hunt," Ellie said.

"That's *if* he gets it tonight," Marshall pointed out. "We all heard him say he'll go until he gets it, and he'll have his buddy guard while he sleeps. We might as well assume he'll still be there tomorrow."

"So we need to stop our parents from going that way," Lydie said.

Everyone nodded. "Now we need to figure out how," I said.

"We'll have to hike through the night," Ellie reasoned. "We're four miles from their campsite, and they plan to be on the trail by seven tomorrow. We either hike now or at two in the morning."

Sawyer nodded in agreement. "And frankly, I'm not comfortable splitting up. I especially don't want the girls to be without a guy."

I inwardly sighed. I was exhausted and hungry enough that I wanted nothing more than to eat and collapse into my sleeping bag. I was not hiding my thoughts well, because Sawyer patted my shoulder. "I know this is hard, Marlee, but we need to do this. It'll be super hard if we try to do it at two a.m. after the adrenaline dies down and we're asleep. We need eat now."

"I second that," I wearily added, remembering Marshall's suggestion to have a snack when we found the rest of our group.

"Hey, how does your face feel?" Sawyer asked.

Shrugging, I said, "It'll go nicely with the scar on my forehead from last summer."

The guys gave half-smiles and Sawyer again patted my shoulder and said, "You're a real trooper."

Since they felt the strongest, Sawyer and Ellie volunteered to cook supper while we three younger hikers rested. Sprawled on the ground, using our packs as backrests, we sat in a semicircle enjoying the smells of supper. It felt so good to have my feet out of my hiking boots for a few minutes. Glancing over to Sawyer and Ellie, I wondered what they were thinking as they worked side by side to prepare our chicken alfredo. The meal would be heavy for our stomachs since we would be hiking again shortly, but we desperately needed the nourishment.

"Marsh," I whispered, and he and Lydie turned to me. "I was pretty freaked out to hear what Thad told his friend about Ellie." Honestly, it made me feel weird. Even though he didn't say it about me, I almost felt disrespected anyway, and I wish Lydie hadn't heard that.

Marshall slowly nodded and whispered back, "Lots of guys talk that way about girls. I can't stand it, but they do. Yeah, guys like good-looking girls, but they shouldn't be selfish jerks." He gave a quiet laugh. "They should be more like me!"

"And smash girls into boulders?" I teased. He half-smiled.

"You and Sawyer aren't like that, though," Lydie said.

Shaking his head, Marshall said, "No, we definitely try to respect everyone...even annoying girls," he teased with a glint in his eye. Then he added, "Although sometimes it is really hard to be around attractive girls and not get distracted by their good looks."

"I don't think Ellie intended to flirt with Thad, and I'm sure she's appalled by what he said. Do you think Sawyer is mad at Ellie?"

"Hmm?" Marshall cocked his head.

"Sawyer's not looking at Ellie with his usual starry eyes," I said.

"He looks tense, too," Lydie said. "And Ellie looks absentminded."

Nodding, I said, "I wish they had a chance to talk this through before the night hike starts."

"Aw, you're overthinking this, girls," Marshall casually said. "If you want my two cents, Sawyer is bugged because Thad was flirting with Ellie. He wasn't happy about Ellie's kindness toward Thad, because Sawyer probably saw all along that Thad was a creep and only interested in Ellie's looks. Eventually they'll talk about it, and it'll all be good again. Right now, though, Sawyer's busy thinking about the night ahead. He's focused. Guys do that a lot. And don't you feel tense and absentminded too?"

I nodded. "That was an informative two cents' worth."

It was perfect timing for the conversation to wrap up, because just then Sawyer said, "Come on over, crew. Supper's ready."

Our chicken alfredo tasted delicious and not a single noodle was left in the pan. I knew that if it was not for adrenaline, we were all tired enough to stay hunkered around the compact camp stove like this for the night. Sawyer set down his bowl and asked me to bring over my camera with the picture of Thad's map again.

"We just need to decide how to bypass Thad tonight without going so far out of the way that we lose precious time and energy," Sawyer said.

"Could we take the Rocky Pass trail that goes to the southwest? It comes out pretty close to our parents," Ellie suggested.

Marshall nodded, and then asked, "But what if Thad sends his friend to scout out all the nearby trails? He already knows we were on top of the ridge."

Sawyer agreed. "My other concern with Rocky Pass is the elevation change. If we go that way, we'll have a two-thousand foot ascent. We're tired enough that we need an easier hike."

"Doesn't the creek where we filtered water go all the way to our parents? Could we walk by that creek?" I asked, pointing to the picture of the map as Sawyer spread out his topo map.

"It does." Sawyer showed us the creek on his large map. "But we'd have to cross the ridge again. And hiking along the creek bed would be pretty rough terrain, and we'll surprise lots of nocturnal wildlife that are there to drink." He paused to consider it for a moment, and then said, "On the other hand, if we hike at the top of the creek bank, it'd be less rocky, and you're right that it would be a mostly direct path. We'll have to fight our way through lots of weeds, but it might be our best option."

"Will we be too noisy blazing off an established trail?" Ellie asked. "The last thing we want is to give away our location."

Marshall agreed. "It's going to be tricky to sneak five people with packs through the dense foliage by the creek."

Sawyer wrinkled his brow in thought. "Well, let's consider Marlee's suggestion to hike right along the water again. There wouldn't be as much foliage to battle, and the sound of the water would mask the noise we make. We'll just have to step extremely carefully. Check every rock before putting all your weight on it, and keep your boots dry so nobody slips."

"Will it be safe to use our lights? What if the treasure hunters come for water?" Marshall asked.

"I think whichever route we choose will be risky. We have treasure hunters, wildlife, and terrain to worry about. We just have to choose the route with the least amount of risk," Ellie said. "I think we should use our lights as much as possible. The last thing we need is another injury. If we get in a spot where we need to be particularly low profile, we'll turn off our lights."

Everyone was silent, listening for Thad and his buddy and trying to formulate a plan. Marshall cleared his throat and slowly said, "Um, Thad obviously knows what Ellie looks like, and Marlee's face looks like she took on a mountain lion."

*Thanks. I love the compliments, Marsh.*

"Uh, sorry, Marlee. It'll fade," he said with an apologetic glance. "And Sawyer took the lead when we helped him, so he'll remember his face too. I think you three need to hide somewhere, and Lydie and I should try to get to our parents. He didn't see *us* very much."

Sawyer looked like he wanted to object, but none of us could really deny that Marshall's reasoning made sense, even if the thought was unsettling. If Thad or his sidekick found all five of us hiking toward "his territory," he'd assume we were after his cache. However, if either of them met up with just Marshall and Lydie, especially if we could disguise them a little bit, they might not realize they're part of our group. Hopefully, Thad was not so paranoid as to think that *every* hiker in these mountains was after his treasure.

"Do you think you can do it, Lydie?" Sawyer and Ellie asked at the same time.

Lydie looked scared, but then swallowed and met Marshall's eyes. "I think I can keep up. Supper boosted my energy. I think I can make it."

"Change into your spare clothes, Lyd," Ellie said. "And let's change up your hairstyle. I'll undo your braid and wrap your hair in a bun near the top of your head, and we can tie my bandana around your hairline to make you look different, and hopefully a little older, than when Thad saw you."

I wondered how Marshall would change his appearance since he has short hair, but Sawyer was already digging in his pack for a long-sleeved gray shirt to loan him. When he put on the sweater, he looked a little bigger, besides wearing a different shirt. I didn't think that was enough of a change, but I didn't have any suggestions given the circumstances. "Put on your beanie, Marshall," Sawyer said.

In a few minutes, Marshall and Lydie both looked marginally different, and they assured us they'd be careful, especially on the ridge. Sawyer gave them a few hurried instructions and then said a quick prayer for their safety. We gave them enough food for each of them to have one meal, just in case. "We're going to find a place to settle down for the night. We won't go far. Here's the satellite messenger in case you have an emergency," Sawyer firmly said, before Marshall could protest. "Take it. Have Lydie carry it if it makes you feel better. I want you to have it along. And, if you do meet up with either of them," Sawyer loudly whispered just before they headed toward the creek, "just comment on the beautiful stars. It's not a lie – just distract them." It was a clear night, and the stars were shining like glitter on a dark canvas. We could hope it would work, but I wasn't confident that star-gazing was a believable enough excuse to dissuade Thad. I didn't have a better suggestion, though.

Ellie and I hugged Lydie, and I bumped knuckles with Marshall. "Please don't let anything happen to her."

He gave a grave nod, and said, "Keep praying." And then they hiked off into the dark.

"Now what?" Ellie asked as we watched Marsh and Lydie disappear.

"Let's hike a quarter-mile or so west and find a place to hide. I think you girls and our packs can squeeze into my tent. I'll keep watch outside the tent, and if Thad or his sidekick finds us, I'll say I have my pack in my tent to keep it dry from the dew, and it seemed like a good night to sleep under the stars," Sawyer said.

"Do we need to disguise you too?" Ellie asked. "Thad will surely recognize you if he leaves his digging to chase us."

Sawyer thought for a minute as we began walking west, and then said, "I can put on my rain jacket. It won't feel too hot with the night temperature up here. Oh, and I can take out my contacts and put on my glasses." I didn't think that alone was a great solution since Sawyer had sunglasses on earlier, but I figured Sawyer probably needed to take out his contacts at night anyway. "Oh! Ellie, I know how much you care about hygiene. You packed an extra razor, right?"

*Huh? What did he have in mind? Wait. He wouldn't -*

"Don't shave your head!" Ellie screeched with alarm.

"No, no, just my whiskers!" Sawyer reassured us both. He did not need a repeat of the botched-up haircut from Marshall. "And I'll have my beanie on. I'll look completely different." Ellie looked skeptical as we walked but didn't say anything. In a few minutes, Sawyer led us into a flat meadow surrounded by trees. "How about here?" he asked. Ellie and I nodded. "Can you girls set up my tent while I take out my contacts? And, uh, do you mind if I use your extra razor, Ellie? I haven't shaved in a couple weeks, so I think my face without whiskers will change my appearance a lot." Ellie quickly found her razor and some lotion to use as shaving cream, since she always packs the bathroom sink. Many hikers would scoff at her backcountry hygiene, but it sure was handy now when we needed to disguise Sawyer!

Our girls' tent is larger than the one Sawyer and Marshall were using for this trip, so it made sense to use his smaller tent. Additionally, his tent was gray, and ours was yellow, so hopefully we'd be less noticeable in his.

Ellie and I worked together, so it didn't take us long to set up Sawyer's tent. We placed our packs inside it and then went to check on Sawyer.

I gasped when I saw thin trickles of blood dripping down his face in four spots, but he shrugged it off, and said, "I always nick myself, especially without a mirror. That's why I don't do this very often!"

Ellie just shook her head sympathetically. "I'm sure you'll get the hang of it soon," she said. I had to admit that with no sunglasses, a beanie covering his sandy-blond hair, and no whiskers, Sawyer did look quite a bit different. I prayed that he looked different *enough*.

Sawyer pulled on his dark green rain jacket as Ellie quickly gathered all our smellables and started stuffing them in our bear canister. When we hike in areas with black bears, we hang food, soap, sunscreen and anything else that smells in a bear bag. In Montana where there are grizzly bears, we were using a sturdy bear canister with a locking lid to deter any hungry visitors. Once all of our smellables were in the canister, we would place it about two hundred feet from our tent.

We were all exhausted, and Sawyer looked nervous. I felt terrified and on edge. "We should pray and then get some sleep," Ellie said. Sawyer and I agreed, and he quietly asked for God's protection for all five of us. After the "amen," he told Ellie and me to try to get some sleep in the tent, and that he was going to settle down a couple hundred feet away from the tent, just to spread us all out in case Thad looked for us here. I did not like the idea of Sawyer sleeping alone without a tent so far from us at the edge of the meadow, but he insisted.

I clumsily lay down next to Ellie and didn't even bother to change clothes or dig out my sleeping bag. Even though I was exhausted, I was so nervous that I didn't think I could relax at all. Ellie curled up next to me, tucked against all three of our backpacks along the side of the tent. It was cozy in the boys' small tent, and I thought about all the awesome places that tent had been.

"Ellie, are you okay?" I asked. She had been unusually quiet ever since we overheard Thad's conversation with his sidekick. "Ellie?" I rolled over and looked at her, surprised that she was already asleep. I didn't think she would fake sleep to avoid talking to me. It was tempting to wake her up to talk. I really wanted to know what she thought about this whole ordeal. Often she and I talk at night, and it's really helpful to hear her ideas and advice. I longed for that during this escapade. Sighing, I realized that what I needed most was to pray to God. I silently poured out my fears to Him, quietly crying and wishing that Thad would just leave us alone.

After a few minutes I felt better. As I noticed the night sounds of crickets, cicadas, and other nocturnal creatures, I felt more peaceful than I had felt since we met Thad that afternoon.

# CHAPTER 8

After rolling over for the sixth time, I sighed and gave up on sleeping. Although I didn't feel as nervous, I really needed to talk to someone. How could Ellie sleep so soundly in these circumstances? I quietly unzipped the tent door, crept out, zipped it back up, and looked toward Sawyer.

Without using my headlamp, I made my way across the meadow, making sure to take a minute to admire the stars. Mom had shown me as a little girl how to find Orion and Sirius and Polaris, and I loved seeing them. Marshall had told me that some people can tell what time it is by using Polaris's location, and I thought that sounded like a cool skill to have. Looking up, I had no clue what time it was – maybe time to learn the Polaris clock trick.

Soon I could see Sawyer's outline lying on the ground next to a big tree, about twenty feet from a small stream. He was on his back with his head resting on his hands and his ankles crossed. It looked like he was awake, but when I whispered his name, he tensed, startled. "It's just me! Marlee," I loudly whispered. He let out a breath. "I'm sorry I scared you," I said. Sawyer sat up and pressed his hands into the grass behind him.

"I'm just jumpy tonight. This whole Thad deal has me really weirded out," Sawyer said, and then asked, "What's up, Mar-Mar?" I smiled when he called me Mar-Mar. Mr. Caleb had given me that nickname when I was little, and it brought back happy memories of family trips together.

"You know me. I couldn't sleep, so figured talking was the next best thing."

Sawyer chuckled. "I feel about the same, to be honest."

"Really?" Maybe he wanted to talk about the news he needed to break to Ellie!

Sawyer nodded. "That Thad thing has me pretty spooked." He had just voiced my own thoughts, and hearing him say it out loud was a bit of a comfort. "Sending Lydie and Marshall alone in the dark to track down our parents before Thad gets there to dig–" he paused with a shake of his head, "I hope it was the right decision."

The thought of my little sister – okay, so she's just a few inches shorter than me, and in my opinion, she surpasses me in wisdom and wit; but that can't change our birth order – needing to face that scuzzy Thad character gave me the chills. I was glad Marshall was with her, and super glad we had said a group prayer before separating.

The more I thought about them hiking through the dark, the more worried I felt. *Time to change the subject,* I decided. "Besides this outrageous situation we're in, what are you thinking about?" *Here it comes,* I thought – well, I hoped. I had just left the door open for Sawyer to tell me about the mysterious news he needed to tell Ellie. *Please take the bait!*

"To be honest, before I fell asleep a few minutes ago, I was thinking about my roommate JJ heading to the Alps this summer. And thinking about JJ reminded me of a funny story," he said as I tried not to look disappointed.

"I like funny stories," I said as I sat down a few feet away facing him.

"Okay, so about six weeks into my first semester at POGS, we had fall break. It's only a couple days, so basically it's a long weekend without class, and everyone who was on trek comes back to base campus. Students who live close to campus go home, others stay at the dorm, and others, like JJ and me, go backpacking."

"What else would you do with a few days off from school?" I teased.

Sawyer chuckled. "Exactly. So, he and I had been planning a three-day trek to summit a peak just an hour's drive from POGS. It's a snowy peak and we were expecting to need our ice axes and crampons. Well, Willow, JJ's girlfriend, was in her whitewater raft guiding class and someone asked her if she was going to meet JJ's family over fall break. A bunch of people from the rafting class overheard her telling about JJ's and my upcoming trek. I was on trail that week for class, but JJ was at the dorm, and when I got back from trek, my phone showed a bunch of group messages from JJ and Willow that thirteen people wanted to join our upcoming trip."

"Talk about inflation." I laughed.

"Yeah, thirteen from the whitewater rafting guide class." Sawyer shook his head with a smile. "Those kids know what they're doing in a river like I know what I'm doing up here. And they're about as experienced with summits as I am on water. None of them had ice axes or crampons, but they were determined to come. JJ and I called every outdoor equipment rental place in the area, and we finally found one store fifty miles away that would let us rent thirteen ice axes."

"POGS doesn't let you borrow equipment?" I asked.

Sawyer shook his head. "Since it wasn't a school-sponsored hike, it would break their policy." I nodded, and he said, "So JJ and Willow picked me up at the climbing gym after my shift there, and we headed to the rental store. It's in the old main street part of town, with a brick road, and there were fancy restaurants nearby. The store was closing in seventeen minutes, and the closest parking space we could find was nine blocks away. Of course, none of us had prepared for a parking meter-"

I interrupted and said, "You are better prepared for the wilderness than for downtown parking."

"Right." Sawyer chuckled. "So among the three of us, we scrounged up enough change to pay for eleven minutes on the parking meter." I laughed, picturing the scene in my mind.

"So we sprinted down the old main street to get to the rental store before they closed and our parking meter expired, weaving in and out of fancy people going to fancy restaurants and shows. We picked up the thirteen ice axes, divvied them between the three of us, and sprinted back to JJ's SUV. We were laughing so hard as the fancy people gawked at us, three people running down the sidewalk with their hands full of ice axes. And we made it back just as the parking meter ran out of time." Sawyer smiled at the memory, and I told him it was a pretty cool story.

He turned to me and said, "What's a crazy story you have?"

"I once survived an avalanche. And met a weirdo treasure-hunter."

"We do have some pretty great stories." Sawyer smiled. "You must have other cool stories too though."

"We went zip-lining last fall," I said. "That was a blast."

Sawyer nodded, "Ellie told me about that day. It sounded like a great time for your family." There was a break in the conversation while I looked up at the bright stars again. Once my eyes adjusted to the dark, it wasn't all that hard to see Sawyer.

I took a deep breath. "Sawyer, what were you trying to tell me a few weeks ago during our webcam chat?"

Even in the dark he made eye contact with me. "Only my parents and JJ and Willow and Marshall know." I wondered if it made Ellie feel left out that Sawyer and his roommate and his girlfriend spent so much time together.

"If you're comfortable telling me, I can keep secrets. Is the news you need to tell Ellie going to hurt her?" My heart pounded as I asked the question. I couldn't stand the suspense.

Sawyer thoughtfully answered, "It won't hurt her, but I don't know if she'll still like me when she finds out." He looked serious and sad at the same time. *What could it be? Better not be Acadia!*

"You can help me figure out the best way to tell her," Sawyer said. "Marlee, I failed a class at POGS, and now I'm on academic probation. That's why I couldn't do an international internship this summer."

I was shocked that Sawyer had failed at anything! Failing a class sure was better than some of the bad scenarios I had been imagining – and it was way better than falling for Acadia – the girl, not the national park. But I didn't get why it was such a big deal. Why would he need to tell Ellie at all? And why did he seem sad about staying in the States?

"If you had gone international, you wouldn't have been able to lead us," I said, feeling slightly betrayed at the thought that he might have swapped his plans with us to go with JJ.

Sawyer shook his head. "Nah, I wouldn't have backed out of the Miles-Stanley trips, but there was a program I applied for that was a six-week gig in the Alps – a shortened version of the program JJ is doing." *What a relief. I knew Sawyer would be loyal!*

"Why do you think failing a class will make Ellie dislike you?"

Sawyer looked at me in surprise, like I should already know the answer. "Ellie's pretty much perfect at everything she does. She's the top of her class at the vet tech program, and uh," he paused awkwardly before continuing, "pretty much a shoo-in for that wildlife program, and she's rocking her studies. I failed Art Appreciation, Marlee. What kind of loser fails art?" he said with disgust.

"Ellie will not think you're a loser or a failure. I mean, maybe if you quit or refused to try again. And besides, it's better to fail art than Wilderness EMT or Alpine Rescue."

"I agree completely, but my advisor doesn't see Art History as dispensable," Sawyer glumly said.

"Why do outdoor guides need Art History?" I pondered.

"Congruent with the mission of POGS, cultural awareness classes better prepare us for life and provide the backbone for a well-rounded education," Sawyer said, obviously repeating a script – probably the same thing his advisor had told him. The way he said it was almost funny, but I forced my amused smile down.

"Can you take it again? Is there a tutor who can help you? Did JJ pass the class?"

"JJ took AP Art in high school so he tested out of Art Appreciation. I can take it again, and it won't even mess up my schedule too bad, thankfully. The tutor is," he paused. "There is a tutor, and – oh, you saw her..."

"Acadia?" I asked.

Sawyer nodded. "Yeah, Acadia is the tutor for *all* of the cultural awareness classes. And I need to pass *without* her help."

"Do you like Acadia?" I braced myself, but I had to find out.

"No, I definitely do not like Acadia like I like your sister. In fact, I barely tolerate her. I mean, she's okay for an acquaintance and a climbing buddy, but she really irks me. Not only is she a flirt – with all guys – she's really nosy and I just don't trust her. She wants to be a kayaking teacher for kids, but –"

"Wait, you don't trust her, but you climb with her?" I interjected. What sense did that make?

"She's a good belayer." Sawyer was referring to the member of a climbing team who is on the ground and uses a friction device to stop the climber from a serious fall. "But I don't trust her friendship. And since we both work at the climbing gym, we inevitably climb together sometimes." There was a slightly uncomfortable pause and then he said, "JJ and Willow and I went climbing a couple times, and uh, we kind of invited Acadia along. But only so we had an even number of climbers. Willow knows her from some of their water classes," he hurriedly added. "Most of the other guys in our class were on trek that week or working."

It was getting worse. I didn't like Acadia. How much time had she and Sawyer already spent together? Why would Sawyer spend time with her if he liked Ellie? Why couldn't the news he needed to tell Ellie be *good* news?

Sawyer saw my face and held up a hand, as if to stop my thoughts. "Mar-Mar, it's not what you think. I *don't* like Acadia, and that's why I refuse to be tutored by her. To be very clear, I already told JJ that next year we need to find someone else to climb with us in her place."

I cocked an eyebrow. "Won't Acadia be jealous? How will you explain to her that you're replacing her role in your climbing team?"

"Marlee, you make it sound like I've flirted with her or asked her out or something," Sawyer said with frustration in his voice. I hoped Ellie couldn't hear us. "I told Acadia I'm interested in someone else – months ago, by the way – but it seems to have fueled her fire to flirt even more."

"So is the news you need to tell Ellie about Acadia or Art Appreciation?" This conversation was not putting me in a good mood.

Sawyer gave me a stern look but patiently said, "I really think that if I don't tell Ellie that I failed a class, I'll feel like I haven't been honest with her."

"But, *why*, exactly? Why not just take the class again, pass it, and move on with life? Do you and Ellie check up on each other's grades?"

Sawyer shook his head. "You know Ellie. She's pretty much perfect, and she expects – and deserves – near-perfection from, um, a boyfriend. I just need to be open with her that I'm not perfect." *As if anyone is, Sawyer.* "And besides, if I didn't tell her, she'd find out anyway when she asks why I'm not going international later this summer. And all the more when she moves for the wildlife vet tech program that's only half an hour's drive from the POGS campus."

*When she moves?! Wait, had Ellie been accepted and not told me?*

I must have looked stunned and worried because Sawyer stammered, "I mean, if and when."

*That makes more sense.*

"So, how do you suggest I tell her?" he quickly asked.

I let out a long breath. I still didn't fully understand why it was such a big deal, but a plan was forming in my mind. "Ellie loves to help people," I began. Sawyer knowingly smiled. "Maybe you could just tell her, face-to-face, that even though you worked really hard, you failed your required Art Appreciation course, and then ask if she could help you pass it next semester."

Sawyer slowly nodded. "That might work. It isn't just memorizing artists and dates and names of masterpieces, though. I could've passed memory work. Instead, I have to write several paragraphs about a bunch of famous artworks, explaining elements of design and what the artist intended to evoke, and how the art makes me feel. Frankly, Salvador Dali's pictures make me feel dizzy! I can't come up with essays about all that stuff!"

I felt sympathetic for his plight, but the way he told the story was almost comical. I couldn't help but giggle, especially when he referred to masterpieces as "stuff." He obviously couldn't fake passion for art.

"Ellie also took AP Art, so she can probably help you figure out what to write. Just be honest with her. Sawyer, Ellie is not going to think you're a failure unless you don't try again. You'd only be a failure if you quit."

He smiled and looked relieved. "Thank you, Marlee. I hope you're right. I really am interested in Ellie. Only Ellie," he clarified, "and I want her to think I'm worthy." His voice had gotten quiet.

"She does," I assured him. Over the past year, Ellie and I hung out a lot. Sometimes I'd ride my bike next to her while she did her running workouts, and other times we'd just chill in her bedroom. While she would sit in her lime-green bean bag chair, I would lay on my belly on her rug with a pineapple design and we would talk – a ton. Dad teased us that we needed to crack a window so we had enough oxygen, but those long talks had really brought us together. A favorite topic of conversation was definitely Sawyer. When they weren't talking to each other, I got to hear all about their conversations, and I knew for certain that Ellie was crazy about Sawyer!

Suddenly I saw a beam of light bounce across the treetops. "Someone's coming!" I urgently whispered.

Sawyer craned his neck to see and murmured, "This can't be good. No way are Marsh and Lydie back yet." He quickly scanned the area as the headlamp beam moved closer.

"Let's get you up in this tree." He stood and jogged to a tree about three feet away. "I'll lay down and look like I'm sleeping under the stars."

*How do I keep getting nominated to climb in the dark?* My heart resumed its fast pumping and my hands started to sweat. Was it Thad or his sidekick coming to chase us? What if the situation became violent? This trip was definitely not turning out like we had planned.

# CHAPTER 9

I stepped into Sawyer's cupped hands with my left foot and he hoisted me up. I had no idea what our plan was, so I silently begged God to plan for us. My hands fumbled along the rough bark of what I assumed was a humongous ponderosa pine tree, since the bark smelled like vanilla. The nearest branch was way above my head, so I had to hug the trunk with my arms and legs and inch my way up like a bear cub. After managing to grasp a branch, I stood and pulled up and then scrambled up a few more branches. "Hide up there, and don't make a sound!" Glancing down, I saw the beam of light bouncing erratically closer to us.

I could barely make out Sawyer's silhouette, now laying on the grass. I wondered if his heart was pounding as hard as mine. The light was darting across the meadow, scanning the whole area. What if it was Thad and he found Ellie in the tent? Why had I left her alone? Or maybe it wasn't Thad or his sidekick at all. Maybe it was just another hiker – though alone and in the dark seemed unlikely.

The swishing of grass grew louder, and I held my breath when I realized that the mystery hiker was nearly upon Sawyer. When the hiker's headlamp illuminated Sawyer, I think I lost two years of my life expectancy from fright. He had been found, and it was clearly Thad's voice that nearly shouted, "You! Wake up! Have you seen five teenagers hiking around here?"

Sawyer squinted and rubbed his eyes and put on a pretty good show of waking from a deep sleep. "Huh?" he asked, confusion in his voice. He probably didn't need to fake the confusion – it was puzzling that Thad would take time away from digging to find us. I was starting to think that everything about Thad was puzzling.

"I'm looking for five teenagers. They were hiking trails along here today, and I need to know where they are," Thad stated in a businesslike tone.

Sawyer shrugged, and uncharacteristically, spoke with a southern accent, "Got lost from your group? I'll keep an eye out for five teenagers, but right now I'm just trying to get some shut-eye under the stars." *What's with the accent?* Then I remembered JJ's Tennessee drawl and realized that must be where he learned how to alter his voice. The guy failed art but apparently he could act!

From my vantage point, I couldn't see Thad's face, but as he shone his headlamp on Sawyer's face, I presumed that Thad was irritated with Sawyer's response. "They're not *my* group, they're thieves!" Thad demanded. *Huh? What is up with this guy?* "Who are you? Why are there so many people in this forest tonight?" Thad angrily asked.

"Well, who are you?" Sawyer stammered.

"Thad. Your turn."

Sawyer paused before plainly saying, "Miles."

"Miles," Thad repeated with a note of skepticism in his voice. "Your name is Miles and you're sleeping in a meadow without a backpack or even a tarp?"

I knew that Sawyer was thinking as fast as he could, and he nodded toward the tent where Ellie slept, blissfully unaware of the confrontation. "My backpack's in the tent," Sawyer cautiously said, still in his fake accent, "but I came out here to see the Milky Way. I can't get over that stripe of light across the black sky." He sure was good at acting casual – well, better than I would be at least! I clung to the tree. Thad shone his light toward Sawyer's tent and glanced around the meadow.

"Stand up," Thad said.

"Excuse me?" Sawyer acted offended. "Just stand up, *Miles.*" *Uh-oh,* I thought, *Thad is going to figure out who Sawyer is.*

When Sawyer stood, Thad eyed him, noting his height and build. *Not good.* Sawyer gulped. "Wait a minute," Thad said, his voice a mix of enlightenment and anger. "Miles. Sawyer. S. Miles. *You're* SMiles on the Trail. You're on *my* trail!" Thad accused. "You're here for *my* treasure!"

"No–" Sawyer started, but Thad interrupted, "Where's the rest of your group?"

Silence. "I asked you, *where is the rest of your group*?" Thad rudely enunciated every word.

*Come on, Sawyer, think.*

Thad's eyes flashed wickedly. "She's in the tent, isn't she? How about the rest of them? Did you send them to beat me to my treasure? You can't fit the other four and all your backpacks in that tiny tent," he observed. "Why did you split up?" Thad was standing close to Sawyer, his accusing eyes glaring into Sawyer's face. They were only about six feet away from me, and I had a pretty clear view between branches.

*Please, God, make Sawyer say the right thing!*

Finally Sawyer spoke, deliberately, but in his usual midwestern tone, "Thad, nobody in my group has any interest in your treasure. None. We came here to hike, because we love Montana and these mountains. Before this afternoon when we helped save your life, I had never heard of you. We didn't know you were looking for treasure until we overheard you on your satellite phone. And the only reason we heard you was because we, the same people who completely changed our plans to save *your* life, were returning a map that *you* dropped when you ditched us at the stream. We didn't take your map. We returned it. We just want to be left alone."

He paused to catch his breath, and Thad prodded, "So why'd you split up?"

"Listen close, Thad, and believe what I tell you. Some more people in our group are on the other side of the ridge. When we saw your map and overheard your digging plans, we realized that the rest of our group is–" he paused, uncertain about how much detail to reveal, "near where you'll be digging. We want you to have your space to dig, because, well, we figure you're a bit like a grizzly bear so we should just stay away." I almost laughed, wondering how Thad liked being compared to a territorial griz. Sawyer said, "So I sent my sneakiest hikers to warn the others to change their plans and give you plenty of space."

"SMiles," Thad sneered, "why did you write that blog post about treasure hunting, in *these* mountains of all places, and why are you here *now* unless you plan to beat me to what belongs to my Grandpa and *me*?"

"I was required to make a blog for a writing class at school, and after running out of post ideas, a friend suggested writing about modern-day treasure hunting. I haven't even thought about that post since the day I wrote it. I came here to hike with my friends," Sawyer tried to reason.

"And you, Mr. Rule-Follower, stayed here alone and sent all the other four to the other side of the ridge?" Thad taunted.

I dreaded to think what might happen if Thad discovered Ellie in the tent. But if I announced my presence too eagerly, that would be even more suspicious. So I did what only made sense, given the circumstances. I sneezed loudly – twice.

Thad's headlamp instantly found me. "Excuse me," I lamely said.

"Who else is up there?" Thad demanded.

"Only me! I mean, only I, to be grammatically correct," I hurriedly said. *Why was I rambling? And who cared about grammar at a time like this?*

"You're the one with the huge gash on her face, yeah? So you and SMiles are hiding out here while the other three hike to tell Part Two of your crew to stay away from me? Did I get this right?" Thad angrily asked.

*Great, I'll forever be remembered as "the one with the huge gash on her face." Wait! He assumed Ellie went with Marshall and Lydie! Awesome!* Sawyer's eyes met mine. I could see that he was scared to death but relieved that Thad thought Ellie wasn't with us. *Us.* What would Thad do to us? Before my imagination could further scare me, Thad spoke again, "Get down." I didn't think it was wise to ignore his order, so I cautiously stepped down the branches, slid down the trunk, and landed on the ground by Sawyer. I felt very small next to this volatile man, even though at five-feet seven inches I don't usually feel tiny!

"Now it's my turn to talk and your turn to listen. SMiles, ever since you wrote your stupid article, people who never before cared about this forest have been coming to explore it – lurking around, asking questions, sneaking into nooks and taking notes. Grandpa and I decided it's now or never. I'm getting his treasure. And guess what? While you were star-gazing I finally found the right spot! Now that I've found it, I'll be busy digging for awhile." Thad dropped his backpack and quickly retrieved something that I couldn't see. "So to ensure that you stay out of my way," he practically pounced on our arms and said, "I'll keep you two right here. Away from my treasure, away from me, and away from Wi-Fi so you can't announce my secret." *Wait, what? Are those handcuffs? What kind of weirdo carries handcuffs in his backpack?*

"I knew these would come in handy," Thad said with a weird smirk. Before I could shout, "*Get your creepy hands off us*," he had cuffed Sawyer's left wrist to my right wrist. I stumbled to the ground as Sawyer jerked back and swung a punch at Thad with his right hand. Thad caught Sawyer's fist like it was a tennis ball and snapped a *second* pair of handcuffs onto his wrist. He shoved Sawyer's back against the tree. As I scrambled to stand, Thad snatched my left arm, twisted it painfully, and cuffed my wrist to Sawyer's. I was speechless! As Thad turned to leave, he scoffed, "Have fun on your hike. I'll check on you in a couple of days."

He grabbed his pack and as he disappeared down the trail, I felt a wave of anger swell inside me, but I was also relieved that he hadn't done anything worse. And I was oh-so thankful that he hadn't discovered Ellie. I briefly entertained myself with the thought that maybe she could even pick the locks on these handcuffs.

I remembered one time Lydie won a pair of toy handcuffs at a circus game. They were totally hokey, but she had so much fun with them. She was constantly playing spy and handcuffing Ellie and me to the railing by our stairs. It didn't take long for us to figure out how to override the cheap plastic locking mechanism and escape those.

Feeling the metal press against the tendons in my wrists, I realized with a sinking feeling that this would not be an easy escape.

At least Sawyer was here though. I mean, seriously, if I had to be on a deserted island, I would absolutely want Sawyer or my dad there to increase our chance of survival. With Sawyer here, the situation didn't seem quite as bleak. Though I would've felt better if Ellie and I were locked, and he was able to move.

"I'm sorry, Marlee. I didn't expect anything like this; and now I don't doubt he has a weapon with him. At first I thought maybe if we showed him we're not a threat, he'd back off. I should have been ready for a fight," Sawyer apologetically said.

"He's like a grizzly bear, and we don't fight grizzlies," I said.

"At least he left," Sawyer pleasantly mentioned.

"And he didn't even take our food," I teased. "I totally should've gotten him with Ellie's can of bear spray."

"Yeah, but then we'd really have to run for our lives," Sawyer said. "Can you imagine if that guy was seriously angry at us?" *As if he wasn't already.* "When he asked my name, I probably should've told him my middle name."

"It wouldn't have worked," I said. "You do not look like an Orville. Thad wouldn't have believed it, and he still would've put the pieces together. And the reason I sneezed was so he would find me and wouldn't look in the tent. Are you mad at me?" I stammered.

"I was so thankful you made your presence known," Sawyer sighed. "Not that I want him to touch you – definitely *not*. But you showing yourself over here by me made him forget that someone might be in the tent."

"Ellie will freak out when she wakes up. Do you think she can break the chains on these with your hatchet?" I hopefully asked.

"I don't know," Sawyer honestly said. "The thought of a hatchet blade coming down so close to our hands is a little disturbing."

"Sawyer…" my voice trailed off.

"Yeah?"

"When we get interviewed by the news for this, will you call me Marlee so the whole world doesn't remember me as the girl with the huge gash on her face?"

"Thad's a jerk. Nobody will think of you that way," Sawyer comfortingly said.

# CHAPTER 10

"Please tell me I have high-altitude sickness and am imagining things," Ellie shrieked. I must have dozed off, because her voice startled me and I jerked my head up. Behind me, I felt Sawyer shift too. Thankfully the tree between us was only about two feet in diameter where our wrists were handcuffed, so our arms weren't stretched out too uncomfortably far. After Thad left us in the night, we had agreed to crouch down, and my head had been resting on my knees, which were still tender from falling on the rocks on top of the ridge the evening before.

"I wish it wasn't real, but I guess since the sun is up and Marlee and I are still handcuffed to a tree, last night's encounter with Thad was not just a bad dream."

"Thad did this to you?!" Ellie continued shouting. "How did I sleep through you two being mauled?"

"Marlee pretty much saved your life, Ellie, and please talk at a normal decibel," Sawyer replied.

Ellie ran to me and squatted down so we were face-to-face. "You protected me? What if he had hurt you?" Ellie's voice was a little quieter, but she was still frantic.

"I was terrified of what Thad might do to you if he found you alone in the tent. When he found Sawyer and me by the tree, he assumed you had gone with Marshall and Lydie. He handcuffed us here *so we can't get his treasure, and he'll check on us in a couple of days*," I sassily mocked Thad.

"Is he going to chase Marsh and Lydie next?" Ellie worriedly asked.

"Didn't sound like it," Sawyer assured her. "When he figured out who we really are, I specifically told him that we only split up to warn the rest of our crew to stay away from him as if he were a grizzly bear. He seemed to believe me on that. Remind me to never blog about treasure hunting again," he disgustedly said. "Or *anything* that might *possibly* involve paranoid weirdos."

"What should I do?" Ellie sounded almost hopeless. She had tears rolling down her cheeks and her hands were clenched into fists at her sides. She looked the same way when we were little and I used all the glittery green paint – furious and sad.

She squatted beside me again and brushed the wild stray hairs back from my forehead. Without a word, she ran to the tent and came back with two water bottles. She held mine up to my mouth and I took a sip. The mountain morning was pretty chilly and I was not thirsty, but even if I had been thirsty, I was getting really worried about what would happen when Sawyer or I needed to relieve our bladders. I'd never thought up a plan for how to pee while handcuffed to a boy and a tree. So I opted for a tiny sip of water, but it was sweet of Ellie to think of us.

Then she stepped around the tree and offered Sawyer some water. "I'll have an ounce," Sawyer said. I figured he was worried about the same thing as me. Next Ellie handfed us each a granola bar after she retrieved the bear canister. It was too bad we hadn't protected ourselves from Thad better. Who would've guessed that a person would be a bigger threat to us than a bear?

I watched Ellie's face closely as she held my granola bar for me. I wondered if she could remember life before I was born. Probably not since she was only two years older than me, but would she miss me if she moved away for the wildlife vet tech program? And what had Sawyer meant when he said "when"? Right then it dawned on me that Ellie had been noticeably silent about the program for the last couple of weeks. Maybe she was rethinking the opportunity and decided to continue her studies close to home in Wisconsin. I hoped so, because looking at her now, I saw a glimpse of how badly I would miss the company of my older sister.

I couldn't think of many memories that didn't include Ellie. She'd always been there for me. There was the time we decided to build a shelter in the woods with sticks. We were convinced it would be so solidly built that in hundreds of years, historians would think ancient Native Americans had made it. We spent days leaning dead tree branches against a fallen log. It was barely big enough for us both to huddle into, but we thought it was the greatest cabin. Then we had the brilliant idea to plaster it with mud. Lydie still napped back then, and when Ellie and I went into the house that afternoon, Mom practically flipped out. *"Get your muddy little bodies back outside!"* I think she had us wash off at the hose before we could come inside. But Ellie was there at my side.

Then there was the time a few years ago when it was my turn to make supper. Cooking is not my forte, and the spaghetti noodles were burned so badly that they pretty much fell out of the pot like a brick. A black brick. I thought Ellie would make fun of me, but she didn't

– well, not at the time. She's definitely teased me about it since, and it's become a joke in the family. But right then, she could see I was embarrassed, so she just grabbed another pot and filled it with water. When Mom came to check on us from folding laundry in the next room, Ellie smiled and said, "I'm just showing Marlee a few tips for the spaghetti noodles." The glint in Mom's eyes told me she knew what had happened, but both of them were really considerate of my embarrassment. Ellie was there at my side.

And who could forget the avalanche? Ellie was right there. Sure she gets moody and her perfectionism drives me bonkers sometimes, but I've always been able to count on her. Lydie and I depended on her so much. Like this – feeding Sawyer and me by hand. I swallowed a lump in my throat as she moved to Sawyer's side of the tree. I didn't want her to move away from home. I didn't want our family to spread out, and I wanted these combined family backpacking trips to continue forever. And I really didn't want to die handcuffed to a tree at the age of sixteen.

"We're not going to *die*," Sawyer's exasperated voice grabbed my attention. I wondered how much conversation I had missed during my daydreaming.

"You could starve!" Ellie countered. "Or a grizzly could come and eat you, or bees could attack and your throats would swell up and you'd both suffocate, or you could get struck by lightning, or Thad could come back with weapons-"

"No." Thankfully Sawyer stopped her, because in case I hadn't had enough worries on my mind, Ellie's list of potential threats gave me plenty to fret over. "We're not going to die, because you can help save us."

Ellie was pacing around the tree but froze in place when Sawyer said she would help save us. "Tell me what to do," she said, determination building in her voice.

"First, let's pray," Sawyer suggested. Sawyer took the lead, and as usual for the past couple years, I was impressed with his maturity as he prayed aloud. It's amazing how chaos suddenly feels manageable after casting our cares on God. Well, at least a little more manageable – handcuffs aside. I was sure glad our rescue wasn't up to us alone!

Sawyer told Ellie, "Get my hatchet from the side of my pack."

*Oh no.* I hoped Ellie's aim had improved since the time she tried to play softball. Based on Ellie's face, she thought the same thing, but she headed to the tent and returned a moment later carrying a hatchet. She didn't look confident as she touched the mere inches of chain between Sawyer's and my wrists. I gulped.

"Can you do it, Ellie?" Sawyer gingerly asked. Ellie stood about three feet from the tree so we could both see her.

Ellie's gaze locked with mine before she looked at Sawyer's face. Her gaze refocused on the very few chain links between our wrists.

I clamped my eyes shut when I saw her wind up like a golfer with a driver club. I held my breath and kept my hands absolutely still and begged God that this moment would end favorably. The moment was dragging on too long. I peeped open an eye and saw Ellie standing in the same wind-up stance. Why was she hesitating? *Just get this over with,* I thought. *Like pulling out a splinter. Just get it over with.*

Suddenly she dropped the hatchet. "I can't do it." Sawyer and I let out enormous sighs. I heard a bird chirp and a squirrel darted past. "I'm sorry, but I can't do it. If I hit your hands, then we have a medical emergency *and* you're handcuffed to the tree..." Ellie trailed off.

"It's okay, Ellie," Sawyer said. "Unless you're absolutely certain that you can hit the exact spot, you shouldn't try." He had a good point. Being stuck to the tree wasn't immediately life-threatening like severed, gaping arteries would be. *But now what?*

Ellie slouched between us a few feet from the trunk of the tree. I could tell she was holding back a sob. I heard Sawyer let out a shaky breath and then timidly say, "Ellie, I know this breaks every rule in backpacking, but I think you need to go find help for us."

Going solo in the backcountry is never recommended, but what other choice did we have? It's not like being handcuffed to a tree is an ideal situation. Marshall and Lydie had probably arrived at our parents' camp already. Supposing our parents and Marshall and Lydie could get to us by late-morning, we would still need professional help to get out of the handcuffs. It's not like we all carry bolt-cutters or angle grinders in the backcountry. *Like I even knew the names of those tools before Sawyer mentioned them.*

Sawyer spoke up, "I just think that realistically our parents and Marshall and Lydie won't get back here until late today, and *then* they'll find us here and call for help, which could take another day or two. And if Thad comes back here for any reason, we could be in serious danger. If he has handcuffs in his pack... well, I don't want him to show up while I'm tied up and you're unguarded. You already checked all our phones for any coverage?"

Ellie nodded and confirmed that our cell phones would not help us here. *Next year we should totally get satellite phones.*

"If you can hike to a high spot with phone coverage, you can call for help so we can get a ranger out here to break these cuffs and detain Thad so he stops threatening everyone. Please bring me the topo map and we'll figure out our GPS or UTM coordinates so you can tell the rescuers where we are." Dad had told me about the Global Positioning System and Universal Transverse Mercator. Both were used in back-packing.

Ellie nodded but asked the obvious question, "What if I run into him?"

"He was set on digging for days, and we know where he's digging since we saw his map. He's in a hurry since he's paranoid that we're after the treasure, so I'm sure he and his sidekick are digging as fast and steadily as they possibly can," Sawyer reasoned. "He thinks you're already with Lydie and Marshall, and I'm pretty sure he believed me that they're simply going to tell our parents to change their hiking plans. He said he'd be back in a couple of *days*, so it's not likely he'll be back today."

"So, as long as I don't search for phone service anywhere near where he'll be digging, I should be safe from him?"

Sawyer levelly said, "You'll go quickly and sneakily, and like a fox, you'll be on the lookout and give him a wide berth if you catch any trace of him, and he'll never know you were there."

There was silence as we let the idea settle. Then Sawyer said, "Ellie, with God, I know you can do it. Take the map and compass and head for high spots, but stay away from the ridge we climbed last evening since it's so close to Thad's location. And it's really dangerous. God helped us hike out of the forest last year. This is just another opportunity to help us build our faith. God allowed this situation to happen, so as long as we're seeking His guidance He'll help us. As soon as you have a bar on your phone, try to call the ranger station." Good thing Sawyer had told us to save that number when we entered the forest!

Ellie returned to the tent and brought back Sawyer's topo map. She knelt next to Sawyer and held the map so he could study it. This was another time when I was so glad that Sawyer had excellent map-reading skills. My skills were improving, but still not great. I heard him murmuring to himself, mentioning a few different landmarks as he narrowed down where we were. I knew that if he could identify our exact location on the map, he could just look to the sides of the map to determine our coordinates, in both GPS and UTM, which should be equally familiar to the rescuers.

However, if he was at all unsure of our exact location, and he probably was a little uncertain, considering that we had gone off-itinerary last night, I knew Sawyer would use triangulation to double-check our location on the map. Triangulation involves finding three obvious landmarks that can be seen, like mountain peaks or ridges, and taking a bearing on the compass. As long as we remembered to adjust for the east-west declination, the difference between magnetic-north and true-north, we could figure out a small triangle on the map where we were. Or more accurately, *Sawyer* could figure it out. I knew the basic steps, but if it were up to me to determine our location, the rescuers might not find us. Good thing Sawyer was along. Sure enough, in a few short minutes he told Ellie which coordinates to tell the rescuers. She used a stub of a pencil that Sawyer kept in his pack to jot the numbers down on the edge of the map.

In the next five minutes, we prayed again as a group, begging God for speedy help out of this unexpected situation. Ellie hugged my head and pulled up the hood of my sweater, though I didn't know why since the day would likely grow warm, grabbed her backpack, and whispered something to Sawyer. I tried to hear what, but only heard fragments about "Marlee" and "tell," whatever that meant. Then she disappeared down the trail. I was alone with Sawyer and my filling bladder. And God, thankfully.

# CHAPTER 11

S awyer and I were silent for several minutes. What does a person
say at a time like that? *"Hey, just wanted to tell you that for my
first-ever handcuffing, I'm sure glad to be chained to you. At least the
ponderosa pine we're stuck to smells good."* Besides, we expected to have
plenty of time to talk, so neither of us was in a rush to start conversation.

What an insane situation. I wanted to punch something. Or cry. I
was distraught, so I rested my head on my knees and let a few exasperated tears spill onto my synthetic trekking pants.

Sawyer's voice startled me. "I should've told her about Art Appreciation before she left."

"Well, time is of the essence," I reasoned, trying to keep the tears out
of my voice. "It'll be better when you have time to explain the situation
more fully to her."

"But what if we do die, Marlee? Or what if something happens
to Ellie?" Sawyer usually was Mr. Calm and Collected, so his voiced
concerns felt like a punch in my side.

"Between you and Ellie listing off all the possible risks, I feel like I'm hearing a list of side effects to a prescription medicine," I said, trying not to freak out.

"Sorry. I've just been worried for weeks how to tell her," Sawyer murmured.

"I think she'll take it well," I said. "I really do. We've spent hours talking to each other this past year, and she really respects you."

Through the handcuff chains, I felt Sawyer straighten up and I could picture his typical confident expression back on his face. "Encouraging people comes naturally to you, doesn't it, Marlee?"

I smiled. "I like to think it comes naturally." I laughed at a random memory. "But not everyone thinks I'm nice."

"What do you mean? Who doesn't think you're nice?" Sawyer asked.

I took a deep, dramatic breath. "Sawyer, this story is kind of crazy, but it really happened."

"I'm all ears," Sawyer said.

"I once gave an Amish guy a black eye," I began.

"No kidding? Why, Marlee? An Amish guy? How did you give him a black eye?!"

I giggled. "Well, you know how there are lots of Amish people near our house in Wisconsin?"

"Yeah," Sawyer said. He had seen their buggies drive past when he and Marshall visited our house to help us plan this summer's trips.

"We buy eggs and produce from some Amish neighbors. Well one day, Mom asked me to run over to their house and buy some eggs. After paying my friend "Egg Emma" – that's what Lydie calls her so we don't get confused with her other friend Emma – for the eggs, I was talking to her for a few minutes. Well, when she went inside, I turned around to go down the porch steps with the eggs. I hadn't noticed her older brother walking up the steps, and he was carrying a wooden crate and could barely see where he was going. I crashed into him, and when we collided, it jammed the wooden crate into his face."

"Ouch," Sawyer groaned sympathetically.

"Yeah, I felt terrible, but he kept telling me that he was okay. But now their whole family teases me about giving an innocent Amish guy a black eye."

Sawyer laughed and said, "That's pretty funny, Mar-Mar. I don't want to be anywhere near you if I'm ever carrying a wooden crate!" We both laughed.

Talking and laughing usually help me feel better. Maybe it was time to breach the subject that had caused me turmoil since it first came to my attention. Maybe talking it over with Sawyer would help me feel better. I could sort out my worries and he could assure me that everything would be just fine. Our talk last night about Art Appreciation had settled many of my worries. It was time to bring up the next worrisome topic.

"Sawyer, has Ellie talked about the wildlife vet tech program in Idaho lately to you? For weeks it was all she talked about, but she hasn't said a word recently. Did something happen to her hopes and plans? Did she not get accepted?"

The silence stretched between us for an agonizingly long time – like probably two whole minutes.

"Sawyer? Are you still awake?"

I heard him sigh and then say, "Yeah, I'm awake. I just don't know what to say."

"Do you hope she doesn't get accepted? Would it be weird for you if she only lives thirty minutes from POGS and wants to hang out but doesn't fit in with you and your friends? Or if you don't fit in with her friends?" I asked. Maybe Sawyer was worried about the possibility of Ellie living relatively near him. They've always had a safe buffer space.

More silence. It drove me bonkers. What was going on?

Then *finally,* Sawyer said, "Ellie does have news about the program in Idaho, and she is waiting for the perfect time to share her news with you. She specifically asked me to not tell you so that she can tell you in her own sisterly way. Try as I may, I can't act like a sister – even though I can mimic JJ's accent pretty well."

So that was what Ellie whispered to him before she departed. Wait, she told Sawyer before her own sister? *Need to cry NOW!*

"When did she tell you?" I whispered.

"Uh," he hesitated and his voice jumped up an octave, "a couple weeks ago. Pretty much the same time I found out that I failed art."

Ellie told Sawyer *weeks* ago and still hadn't said anything to me?! I hated feeling left out. That's when I realized that I still didn't know what the news was, exactly. Maybe the news was that she wasn't moving halfway across the country. A girl could hope! But I needed to know.

"What *is* her news?"

"She asked me not to tell you." *Loyalist.*

"If she's upset that you told me, we'll just tell her that I got you handcuffed to a tree and forced the truth out of you," I suggested.

Sawyer sighed behind a chuckle and then gently said, "No. She needs to tell you herself."

Tears flooded my eyes. My throat felt huge and I could feel my pulse in my forehead. It must be that Ellie would be leaving home.

After a few minutes of listening to me cry – and no, I wasn't trying to guilt him into telling me by letting the very real tears fall – Sawyer quietly asked, "Is there anything I can say to help you through this?"

He's the big brother I've always dreamed of having, in addition to my sisters, of course. "When is she moving? When is she going to tell Mom and Dad? Who can possibly expect me to act as the oldest sister when she's gone? What will I do at night when I need to talk to her? And when are you two getting married?!" I deluged him with questions between sobs. I totally surprised myself with the last question, but since it was already out there, I might as well find out.

Sawyer took a breath, and in his usual orderly manner, said, "Her program begins the day after Labor Day, so she plans to move during the last week in August." *As in six weeks from now?!* "She told your parents before she told me." *Again, that horrible feeling of exclusion.* "You've already been an older sister to Lydie for years, so you have lots of practice at being the older role model. As far as being the old*est*, I am sure you'll step into the role gracefully." *Hopefully more gracefully than when I've fallen off a horse at riding lessons.* "You and Lydie are also growing up, so you don't need Ellie in the same ways you needed her as a little girl." *Oh really? How can you assume that? YOU wouldn't know, Mr. Firstborn. You SHOULD know that I DO need her really badly. You should know that younger siblings need their older siblings.* "When you need to talk to her, she'll only be a phone call away." *Except that she'll have a rigorous work and school schedule and we'll probably just play phone tag. And texts are SO not the same as her voice.*

"And?" I urged.

"And what?" he tried to sound naive, but I knew he remembered the last question I posed.

"When are you and Ellie getting married?" I plainly asked, and then for encouragement, which comes naturally, I charismatically said, "Since we're talking about short and long-term goals, I'd like a little clue as to when you'll officially be my brother."

"Nobody said anything about long-term goals," Sawyer playfully said.

"I did."

Sawyer chuckled and said, "I need to finish my training and start making enough money to buy her a ring and earn a living before I can propose. And there's always a chance that we won't get married after all. I mean, I sure hope we will, but we don't know the future, and we haven't said 'I do' yet." *As if she'd say no.* I mean, for years they couldn't stand each other, or so they pretended, but since last summer, they've been all starry-eyed at each other. Totally cute.

"But assuming you do marry each other, when will that be?"

"Well the program I'm enrolled in at POGS is two and a half years, and I just finished the first–"

"You're marrying my sister in one and a half years?!" I interrupted in shock. I mean, it's not like I didn't want them to get married, but thinking of Ellie moving away in six weeks had interrupted those good thoughts.

Sawyer sighed, sounding a little exasperated. "Marlee, nothing is set in stone. A year and a half would be the absolute soonest, and that's pretty unlikely since I won't be making money yet. Kids grow up and get jobs and get married, and you and Lydie are growing up too. Ellie has been begging God to open the door for this internship." Sawyer was right. I needed to support Ellie in this and encourage her to take the opportunity – too bad it was a thousand miles away.

Sawyer took a big breath and said, "Marlee, you know what you need to do?"

"What?"

"You need to talk to Marshall," he said in a clear tone. It didn't sound like a suggestion.

"Why?" I wondered.

"Marshall has already dealt with me leaving home. He and I are pretty close too, like you and Ellie, but in a manly way—"

"What's 'in a manly way'?"

"A little less talking and giggling, but still close," he explained, though I didn't really understand. "Anyway, Marshall and I are close, and we've stayed close even while I'm at POGS. And he's figured out how to keep busy without me at home. And he's figured out how to order double portions when our parents take him out to eat without me." He laughed. It was enough to make me giggle.

It was my turn to be silent, not knowing how to voice my thoughts.

"What is it, Mar-Mar?" Sawyer carefully asked.

It was one of those times when I thought out loud, almost as if my thoughts weren't organized until I heard them, and then it all made sense. I quickly and very ungracefully said, "It's just that if I talk to Marshall, we might get close. To each other, you know. And then if our friendship gets any closer than it's been this past year," because truthfully, Marshall and I did talk *some* even between the boys' visits to plan, and I did consider him a friend, probably the closest guy friend I had, "but he winds up liking – you know, *like* liking – another girl, I would miss our friendship. And so I can't get closer to Marshall, or any guy, but especially not Marshall, because if he breaks my heart, our family backpacking trips would be forever changed. I really don't want to lose him as a friend," I stammered.

"Like that Bentley guy?" Sawyer quietly asked.

"Even you know about Bentley?" I asked in dismay. How embarrassing.

"What do you mean that *even* I know? Our families are best friends, Marlee. I was really sad for you when that happened, and mad at him for how he treated you. Any good guy knows you don't dump a girl to date her friend," Sawyer said kindly.

"Sierra Wainwright is *not* my friend," I muttered. Even though it still hurt to think about, I considered myself mostly over The Bentley Drama, as Ellie named it. It no longer stung so bad to see Bentley and Sierra together, and it had happened over a year ago, so I was used to not talking to Bentley all the time anymore. I didn't miss his friendship as much now as when he first switched his interest from me to Sierra in the blink of an eye. We hadn't actually dated, like Sawyer implied, but we had been really close friends, and I liked him a lot. I thought he liked me as much  – that is, until I saw him and Sierra sharing a malt at Here's the Scoop in a booth by themselves.

If I gleaned nothing else from the experience, I hoped to be able to warn Lydie to not get attached to a guy until she was absolutely certain that their ideas for the relationship aligned. Ellie told me my adverse side effect from The Bentley Drama is that I'm very hesitant to trust people – guys because they might break my heart, and girls, because they might swoop the guy I like away right before my eyes. Frankly, I don't think being hesitant to trust is 100 percent *adverse*. But Ellie is older and wiser, and I figured I had better listen closely to her for the day when Lydie comes to me for advice. Hopefully Lydie will take the safe route and just call Ellie, who apparently would be leaving home very soon. When was Ellie planning to tell me, anyway?

Good thing Sawyer interrupted my thoughts. "Marlee, I'm just saying" – *oops, had he been talking?* – "that Marshall is not going to hurt you like Bentley. He'd probably like to talk to you about adjusting to life when an older sibling moves away for school. Pretty much the only people he talks to are the kids he jams with. He could use a conversation with you. He thinks you're pretty cool."

"The kids he jams with?"

"Yeah, Marsh plays guitar and drums. Several of his buddies do too. They always come over to our house and Mom puts in her earplugs while they jam. I mean, they sound good, just loud in the house, you know." I hadn't known. Marshall had never told me he was a musician. I couldn't say why it bothered me to not have known that fact about Marshall. Maybe because we had survived an avalanche together, and just hours ago we free-climbed a dangerous rock face in the dim light to escape a dangerous guy. Or maybe it bothered me because again I felt excluded, that if not for Sawyer I would be totally out of the loop. Good thing Sawyer had my back. Who would've guessed that being handcuffed together would have a silver lining?

# CHAPTER 12

Considering Ellie had left us over an hour ago, I estimated, I would've thought the sky would be brighter. I must have dozed through the sunrise, so I couldn't use the color of the early morning sky to predict the day's weather. *Red at night, Sailor's delight; Red in the morning, Sailor take warning,* Mom and Dad always said. It was definitely daylight when Ellie had found us and later departed, and usually the sun rises into the sky pretty quickly. The clouds seemed low and dark, but maybe they just looked that way since our elevation was high here, about nine-thousand feet above sea level. I hoped we didn't get rained on. Sawyer at least was wearing his rain jacket. I still had on my fleece sweater, so at least if it did rain we were decently dressed for it.

"So, Mar-Mar," Sawyer said, "do you know what you want to do after high school?"

I dread that question. I mean, I'm sixteen, not a prophet. But everywhere I go, everyone wants to know my plans for the future. If only I had a clue. Some people, mainly Ellie, are so confident and driven and formulate and stick to their plans for the future. Me, on the other hand, well, I pray that God will make my future clear, but I really don't have a clue what to do after earning my high school diploma.

My mom is a stay-at-home mom, even though I think her title should be race-around-and-keep-the-family-and-home-running-efficiently-and-lovingly mom. Maybe I should ask her what she did before Ellie was born. Funny, I've always thought of her as a mom, and didn't even bother to wonder what she did before she and Dad had us. Hmm, maybe talking to Mom would help too.

"You have time to decide, Marlee. I was just curious and thought it might be a good conversation," Sawyer said after my silence. That's the other thing. People always ask me what my plan is, and then they quickly tell me I have *so* much time to decide, but a minute later they tell me that life flies by faster than a blink. I really dread the "after high school" conversations. Why can't everything just stay the same? Ellie and Lydie and I can keep living with our parents, eating at Here's the Scoop after church, and talking at bedtime. I wouldn't mind a lack of change.

"Maybe you'd be a good occupational therapist," Sawyer suggested. "You're certainly kind enough to people." That's an idea I hadn't considered before. "Keep tossing out your suggestions, Sawyer. I need all the inspiration I can get."

"Or if you want less college time, you could go to a tech school," he suggested. *That only narrows my options down to five-thousand,* I thought with a hint of sarcasm as I recalled the lengthy lists of degree options that tech schools offer. Really, though, I did appreciate his ideas. Maybe if we kept talking, we could select a few options and I could be more confident and driven, like Ellie.

"Do you have specific suggestions?" I asked.

"There's always POGS, and there are tons of job opportunities in the outdoors. Or if you want to stay closer to home, you could become ...uh, an instrument repair person."

"Instrument repair?" That could be interesting. Although it made me feel guilty about the dusty violin case on my shelf, and the piano lessons that I hadn't finished.

"Yeah, you could learn how to fix all the musical instruments. Or you could be a dental hygienist, or a photographer," Sawyer rattled off. I wondered if I could work outdoors like him. Talking with Sawyer about the future made it seem less scary.

"Basically, Marlee, I would just encourage you to take life a day at a time, and keep track of what you enjoy. There's no rush. People, even those people who seem so confident to you now, change careers all the time. Just keep praying, try a few different part-time jobs and job-shadow some people, and you'll be just fine. Maybe take an aptitude test. For now, enjoy your time with Lydie and your parents. God will direct your path, Marlee."

"Hey Sawyer," I said.

"Yeah?" he asked.

"Thank you. I really needed to hear that," I quietly said.

"I know," Sawyer gently said. I sighed contentedly, silently thanking God for Sawyer's brotherly kindness.

A jolting thunder crack made us both jump. I looked up to the sky, trying to gauge the clouds. "Hey Sawyer, which direction am I facing?"

He thought for a second and said, "You're facing north."

"That's what I thought too," I murmured, concerned by the billowing thunderheads. Dad always said that while weather generally comes from the west, storms often swoop in from the north – especially substantial thunderstorms. Apparently I hadn't noticed the weather build up during my lamenting over the future. I should've been paying more attention to the very-near future! Though I'm not sure what I could have done even if I had been watching the weather.

"How bad does it look in the north?" Sawyer asked as a strong and chilly wind rushed into my face and made me shiver.

"Let's just pivot around the tree so you can see for yourself. I'd put more stock into your meteorology report than mine," I said. We inched our feet sideways, at first going toward each other, and then both awkwardly going the opposite way. When our handcuffs again painfully pressed on our wrists, Sawyer took charge.

"Okay, on the count of three, start stepping to the right," he suggested. That plan worked, and in a minute we had switched stations with each other and Sawyer gave a low, "Whoa, that looks like a big storm. Did it just come over the ridge, Marlee? The clouds are definitely moving fast, and those white clouds look like they might drop hail on us."

To emphasize his point, a flash of lightning illuminated the whole meadow. "Sawyer, are we at high risk for being struck?" I screamed in fear. *God, please do not let us get fried by lightning! We're too young to have our brains and bodies blasted with electricity!*

"Well, I'm sure glad there are other trees near us, but I'd feel better if we weren't attached to metal. What kind of paranoid freak hikes around handcuffing people to trees?!" Sawyer echoed my thoughts.

"Marlee, we really need to pray." I agreed, and he took initiative to start. "Father God, we beg you to protect Marlee and me from this storm right now, and please keep Ellie safe wherever she is as she races to get us out of this situation, and we pray that Marshall and Lydie are safe with our parents." He paused then and I wondered if he meant for me to take a turn praying aloud. Before I could start though, he said, "And God, we also ask that You will soften Thad's heart toward us and resolve this whole misunderstanding. And even if Thad goes down fighting us, help us to shine as lights in the world and honor You. Even more than our physical safety, we ask for spiritual safety – that we will make choices that will please You, even though we're mad enough at Thad to – um, make choices that would not reflect Your light. This is going to take more strength than we imagined. In Jesus' name, Amen."

Did I mention that I love when Sawyer prays aloud? He and Lydie both have the ability to talk so honestly to our heavenly Father, and it totally inspires me. I mean, I pray too, but sometimes my prayers sound a little like a grocery list of concerns followed by, 'Oh, thanks for this, and that was totally inspiring when You did that. But I also want..." When Sawyer and Lydie pray, their words roll out like a beautiful mountain stream, just crystal clear and honest and heartfelt. And when I hear them pray on our behalf (which has happened *a lot* during last summer's and this summer's hikes), I actually feel strengthened by God. It's totally cool.

Something Sawyer prayed really caught my attention – that we would be spiritually safe. Often I find myself very concerned about physical safety, but he's so right that our spiritual state is more important than our physical state. Even if we do get struck by lightning, would I still praise God? Or would I give up on God? Then I thought of Job in the Bible and all the horrors he endured and how even though he was frustrated with God (who wouldn't be?), Job still admitted that God deserves all the praise in the world. Hmmm, the thoughts made me realize that I should continue to pray for my spiritual strength more than my physical strength.

BOOM! Another thunderclap filled the meadow, startling me from my thoughts. "How does the sky look now, Sawyer?"

"Ominous. Threatening. Like a deluge of rain and hail is going to crash down on us momentarily," he said nervously.

*Well then. Let's aim for spiritual safety and pray that the physical pain is not more than we can endure.*

I knew that the weather in mountainous areas can change faster than my preference when I'm picking ice cream flavors at Here's the Scoop. When our elevation is at cloud-level and the terrain of the mountains shifts wind patterns, storms can easily brew up – and when I am stewing about my lack of post-high school plans, storms can brew up before I even notice anything is wrong!

I guess in a way maybe that's a life lesson, too. Ellie is a recovering perfectionist, as we affectionately tease. She has the best of intentions in her attention to detail, but as Dad has reminded her in the past, sometimes she can't see the forest for the trees. There was the time our two families had taken a short canoe trip together on a little river about halfway between our houses. Ellie, Lydie and Sawyer were in one canoe together. Marshall and his dad and my dad were together, and I was with Mom and Ms. Julia. Anyway, Sawyer announced that we all needed to *deliberately* flip our canoes over to practice what we would do "in the unlikely event of a capsize." Mr. Caleb and Dad looked amused but didn't argue with his reasoning. Then without warning, Sawyer pulled on one side of the canoe with enough force that it flipped. Lydie laughed as she dove into the water, but Ellie came up spluttering, "My flip-flop! Grab my flip-flop before it drifts away!"

As she swam after it, Sawyer disgustedly said, "Who cares about your ninety-nine-cent flip-flop? You should've worn practical close-toed water shoes! Help me grab the canoe before it fills with water and gets insanely heavy!"

The rest of us were laughing our heads off, because it seemed silly that Ellie's priority was her missing flip-flop rather than the canoe. But this time, I was guilty of being so caught up in how to map out my future that I didn't see a massive thunderstorm approaching over the mountain ridge until the thunder shuddered right through my body. I know Ellie's missing flip- flop wasn't as important as planning for the future, but the memory made me realize that I had been focused on the wrong details and totally missed the storm arising.

Maybe that's why the Bible tells us to seek God's Kingdom more than anything else in life. It's so easy to be concerned about all the details, like where to schedule college visits and what to wear to church and what to say to Bentley and Sierra when they ask how I'm doing (while they're holding hands, by the way). But maybe all those details in life are just that – details. Distractions. Distractions from keeping my focus on God's plan. Obviously, many details do matter, but our main focus should be on God's plan. In this case, details distracted me from seeing a big storm coming my way. If I allowed everyday worries to take over my thoughts, what other storms might I not see coming? What spiritual storms might approach and threaten my faith? I knew then that it was time to start seeing the forest, not just the trees.

Just then a whoosh of rain pelted down. If clouds had trap doors, the massive slate-gray clouds just opened theirs. Thankfully the needles on the pine tree would provide us some protection from the rain, but I knew it was just a matter of time before we still got soaked. I was so glad that I happened to have on a fleece sweater, keeping at least my head and torso dry. *Wait a minute!* That was why Ellie had covered my head with my hood. She must've seen the clouds and realized we may have rain! She knew I wouldn't be able to put my hood on with my hands cuffed to Sawyer's by the trunk of the tree. I knew, too, that had she not covered my head, hypothermia would set in much sooner. *Thank you, God, that Ellie saw this coming and helped me!*

"Mar," I heard Sawyer shout above the noise of the blasting raindrops, "on the count of three, let's step to the right again so neither of us is facing straight north. It'll help if only our sides and not our faces take the full force of the wind and rain." *Oh, poor Sawyer! He must really be getting bombarded with the rain on the other side of the tree!*

As we shuffled our feet around the base of the tree, I felt the force of the rain as my shoulder and side drew toward the winds racing out of the north. "I'm sorry, Sawyer!" I shouted, "I'm sorry your face got hit with this!"

"Thanks for being willing to share the impact!" he called back. This was one of the biggest storms I'd been in so far. I just kept praying that we wouldn't get struck by lightning. I felt a wave of relief each time a bolt struck somewhere away from us. The lightning was coming about every three or four seconds, and the thunder was nearly a continuous rumble. I was glad for my waterproof hiking boots, but the rain was running down my body and legs and filling in from the top. Waterproof boots are only waterproof until the water floods over the top.

My teeth were chattering, but I think that was more from adrenaline than cold – so far. Hopefully the sun would come out shortly after the storm to warm us and keep us from getting hypothermia.

Just then an animal nearby caused us both to look to my left and Sawyer's right. When we snapped our heads to see, a cinnamon-colored grizzly bear galloped by, about thirty feet from us. The huge bear was running uphill. I was thankful for the distance between us – just in case. We couldn't exactly play dead while handcuffed to a tree with our faces and internal organs vulnerable to three-inch claws. I've never been threatened by a griz, but I knew what to do should it ever happen. If threatened by a black bear, fight back. Dad and Mom taught us girls that as one of our earliest lessons. Seriously, I'm pretty sure they taught us that right after we were potty-trained. But grizzly bears are a totally different story from gentle blacks.

*"If a grizzly bear threatens you,"* I could hear my Dad seriously explaining, *"lay on your belly with your feet stretched out like an X and*

*your backpack on your back. Cover your neck and spinal cord with your hands, and keep your non-dominant hand on top. Laying flat and wide will make it a little harder for the beast to flip you over and damage your eyes and organs."*

It's not one of those scenarios that's pleasant to think about, but Dad has always insisted that we practice so that way, if we were ever threatened, our instinctive response would be the safest response. Anyway, as I saw the muscled bear rush up the hill, I was glad to appreciate the animal's strength and surprising beauty from a safe distance.

The rain continued to pour down, and in the distance I could see Sawyer's tent taking a beating in the wind. Last night when Ellie and I pitched it, we almost considered leaving off the tent fly since the sky was clear. Good thing Dad had taught us to err on the side of caution! Even with the rain fly on, at this point I knew there would be at least some water inside it. Good thing it was several hundred feet away from the stream.

Just then, a mother moose and her calf bolted past us. It was cool to see the little moose, with its gangly legs and proportionately-large head, scamper alongside its mother to keep up. It was probably only a couple of months old but was able to run almost as fast as his mom. God's creations are so expansive and amazing.

"Marlee!" I heard Sawyer call through the storm as another clap of thunder echoed through the meadow. "I saw the moose too!" I called back.

"No, Marlee!" he shouted, just as a fox darted past, following the path of the moose. *The fox has no chance of catching a moose calf for lunch,* I thought. Why would a small fox even consider taking on a mother moose, one of nature's fiercest mammals, to wrestle her baby who is still four times the size of the fox? The blinding rain was making it harder to see, though, so I closed my eyelids against the pelting rain for a minute.

Then I heard Sawyer shout, "The stream, Marlee!"

*Huh?* I'd been so busy watching the wildlife that I'd forgotten about the stream. Cautiously turning my head to the right, my eyes must have almost tripled in size when I saw the stream. Previously the slow-moving mountain creek had been about twenty feet away from our ponderosa pine. However, with this downpour, the stream had erupted into a raging whirl of fast-moving water. The banks of the water were visibly increasing as I stared in fear. Right then, the water was only about five feet from our boots. Four-and-a-half feet. Four feet! I'd never seen a flash flood before, but watching the water rushing toward us gave me a glimpse of why they're so dangerous.

"Marlee!" Sawyer's voice cut through the roar of rain and river, "Put the bottoms of your feet against the trunk of the tree. We have to go up!"

There's a new idea – climbing while handcuffed. Our trip was changing plans so often that I felt dizzy just thinking about it.

# CHAPTER 13

S ome people say that they work best under pressure. Others do better with time to prepare and think through a fully-baked plan.

It's no secret that Ellie has always been the fully-baked plan kind of girl, whereas Lydie seems happy as a lark to improvise and go with the flow when needed. I've never really known if I work better under pressure or with no pressure. I mean, I saw the importance of planning our itinerary well in advance for our return trip to the mountain where we survived the avalanche. Months before our trip, we had to obtain permits, and in the weeks before, we had to prepare lots of food to take in our backpacks. We needed to get fuel for our stoves and check through all our gear, from socks and boots to backpacks and tents. There's no way we could've had a successful trip without tons of planning. And I sure wouldn't have wanted to try!

On the flip side though, last night we decided we had to split up and Marshall and I had to free-climb the ridge. I'd never really free-climbed before, or wanted to for that matter, but when I absolutely needed to,

I made it! I was proud of my accomplishment. It made me think that maybe I do work well under pressure, because no way would I have planned to do that!

But when Sawyer told me we would need to climb the ponderosa pine tree while handcuffed to escape the flash flood, I was stunned. And while I sure hoped I could work well under pressure again, I *almost* laughed and said, "*Why not?! Let's do this!*" It would become a moment of sink or swim, though at least we didn't need to worry about being swept away since we were secured to a massive tree. *But we could get pulled under and drown!* I took another glance toward Sawyer's tent and saw that it was still a couple hundred feet from the river, so God willing, the tent and all our gear would be secure.

"Are the soles of your boots against the trunk?" Sawyer shouted.

"Yes," I called back.

"Press your palms against the sides of the tree and scoot your feet up as high as you can, then push up with your legs. Use the counter-pressure of your hands and back to your advantage," Sawyer coached. He had to shout to be heard over the roar of the river and the rain still pounding down.

With all my strength, which wasn't feeling like much at that point, I did what Sawyer said. My fingertips gripped the bark, my ankles were stretched way beyond their comfort zone, and I pushed up with my legs. It was pretty cool that the method worked, and we hauled our bodies up the tree, our backs scraping against the tree trunk the whole way. I hoped Sawyer's rain jacket wouldn't tear from the friction of the tree, but nothing could be done to help that.

I guessed we were about eight feet up when the river swallowed the base of the tree. I could actually feel the whole tree jolt when the water first crashed around the trunk. It was murky and swirling fast, full of tree branches and medium-sized logs. I could feel Sawyer's handcuff links tugging on my wrists, so I knew that he was still going up. My thigh muscles were trembling, and I was afraid my boots would slip on the wet bark. If I slipped, it would pull down Sawyer, and we would probably drown. The water was still rising, along with my frantic heart rate.

The avalanche had been over in a few seconds, but this flash flood had already been going for several minutes, and there was no sign of it letting up. Taking a deep breath, I forced my legs and feet to cooperate and scoot my body up again.

Suddenly I saw antlers in the river, bobbing up and down. I screamed and shouted Sawyer's name. As the antlers rapidly swept past us, about seven feet away from us, I could see that the antlers belonged to a deer, maybe a mule deer. He was flailing his legs, trying desperately to survive, and it reminded me of myself in the avalanche last summer. He lunged his head above the water for a second, visibly taking a gulp of air before being yanked under again by the force of the flood. In that moment, watching the deer fight for his life as we were comparatively safe above the water, I began to realize the level of danger we were in. I know the deer is just an animal, but in the second that I could see the head, his eyes showed panic. I gulped back a sob and suddenly felt sick. That could easily have been us, frantically trying to keep our heads above the raging river.

I remember a similar feeling of humility when we began to see the effects of the avalanche last summer. Nature is so much bigger and more powerful than people. It only takes minutes of being buried under snow or held under water to die. One forceful hit in the chest from a falling boulder could be the end. It's really sobering. And each time I think of it, I thank God that He is in control and loves to work miracles. If I spend time worrying about every little risk, I'd go crazy, so I try to just leave it to God.

"Sawyer, let's pray!" I called.

No answer. He must not have heard me, so I called louder, "Sawyer, I think we need to pray again! We should ask God to make the flood go down. And to send the hail somewhere else so we don't get hit with that too."

That's when I heard Sawyer gasp for air and felt the handcuffs pulling me down. My back was suddenly scraping down the trunk of the tree and the handcuffs wrenched on my wrists. "Sawyer, what's wrong?" I screamed. After we'd made it this high up the tree and this long in the flood, how could we fall now? My heart drummed in my head and chest and I screamed at Sawyer not to die or drown or fall down the tree. I don't know what else I shrieked, but I was terrified. I wished I could see what was wrong with Sawyer. Or maybe I didn't want to see. Knowing what was happening might paralyze me with fear. Definitely not time for that. I needed to act.

I yanked my wrists up, jamming the metal cuffs into my tendons, making me wince. I drove my feet into the trunk of the tree and refused to let my back slip farther down the bark. "Sawyer, are you okay?" No response, so I used every ounce of fierceness I could summon to drag myself up again. It hurt so bad that I was pretty sure my wrists would snap any second. I couldn't believe the force of the flood.

Finally, *finally* the pressure of the hand cuffs relaxed, and I heard Sawyer cough and the chain links clank as he worked his way back up to my level. "What happened?" I demanded. "You scared me to death!"

"I'm so sorry, Marlee! Did you see that hunk of tree coming at us?" I let out a huge breath when I heard Sawyer's voice again.

"No, I was watching that deer," I answered.

"On my side a huge tree branch rushed right past me, and the sticks and leaves hooked my boot and started pulling me away and under the water. My body was completely off our tree before the branch got untangled from my leg. How did you hold us both up, Marlee? I thought we were goners," he soberly said.

I felt like the air was forced out of my lungs as I was hit with the realization that at the very moment I was feeling thankful that God works miracles and said we should pray, God was already a step ahead of me and diving in to save our lives – again! We were keeping Him busy.

"The rain is slowing down!" called Sawyer. *Phew.* "You okay?"

"Just shaken up," I answered, determined not to cry. Emotional times like these often make me cry, and even though Sawyer had seen me cry a few times before (okay, plenty of times), I didn't want him to know I was crying.

"It's okay to cry, Marlee," Sawyer said. *How did he know?!* "This is pretty terrifying, especially when we don't even know where the other three are." They probably weren't even aware there was a flood in our meadow, and maybe had even escaped the thunderstorm. Mountain weather can be spotty. "Marlee, I know you think I'm all tough and confident, but really, you don't have to be embarrassed to cry. You're not even in front of me this time," he gently teased.

It was enough to make me smile through my tears. "Will you brag about this to JJ?" I wondered aloud as the rain lessened to a sprinkle. What a change from the relentless downpour.

"I sure will," Sawyer confirmed. "I really wish he could have seen us shimmying our way up the tree as the flood encompassed the trunk. Someone should write a book about this. Or make a movie, but only if they could make it look realistic like what we actually lived through." He paused for a minute and quietly added, "But don't get me wrong, I'll spend the rest of my life thanking God for keeping us safe, and I'll tell JJ that it was one of the most dangerous situations I've experienced, and that you started to pray right when the tree branch entangled my boot and dragged me away, and that God saved us."

I let Sawyer's vivid description sink into my mind. My leg muscles ached and I really wanted the water level to descend quickly so we could rest, but even though the rain had stopped, the river was still deep and moving fast. I glanced upward and saw a branch just above us, but there was no way we could get onto it with our arms hand-cuffed behind us.

I asked Sawyer to pray again, and he did, and then I said, "Tell me a story to get my mind off my aching legs and wrists. Or better yet, answer a question," I suggested.

"Nothing about Rembrandt, please, but ask away. Whew, this is a good workout for the quads. I'll tell JJ since he's always looking for new ways to work out." *As if professional backpackers need to exercise more...*I shook my head in wonderment. I consider a day of backpacking to be enough exercise for a day, but Sawyer and JJ probably finish a day of backpacking with push-ups and burpees.

"During our webcam chat, Acadia said something about bicycling across the country and free solo climbing," I ventured to say.

"And your question is?" Sawyer hesitantly asked.

"Fill me in, please. Are you really going to bicycle across the country and do free solo climbing?" I asked worriedly. I think Sawyer was picking up on my apprehension toward Acadia and therefore, he felt nervous every time I brought up her name. But I had to know what was going on, with Sawyer and with flirty Acadia. I was also worried about his safety, so of course I wasn't crazy about him free solo climbing either. I just didn't like that *Acadia* was worried for him. She needed to find someone else to worry about.

"Marlee, I need to set you straight." *Gulp.* "Acadia *thinks* she's a close friend of JJ's and mine, but she isn't. She hears a little rumor and then acts like an expert who needs to give us advice. We really don't like to spend much time with her, and thankfully, next semester we won't have any classes together. I'm praying she'll pick a new first-year guy to irritate and will forget about me. Willow and JJ are also pretty annoyed by her lately. So, I promise you that Acadia is not on my radar. I have zero interest in her. Only your sister."

*Phew.*

"And the rumors she alluded to also shouldn't scare you. See, that's what I mean about Acadia. She tried to act like she was all involved with my plans and my life in front of you when she's not. Anyway," he gave a little huff, "one day at the climbing gym where JJ and I work, we were playing around in the bouldering cove, and he had memorized a route and wanted to try it blindfolded."

"Wow, that would take so much work!" I was impressed.

"Yeah," Sawyer agreed, "and when I applauded his ability to memorize every hold for the route, he told me that he had heard that the famous free solo climbers, you know, like Alex Honnold, memorize the route and practice each move extensively before trying a big climb without ropes. So I was telling him, 'JJ, you're like Honnold,' because I was pretty much in awe to watch him climb blindfolded. And just as I said that, Acadia walked by and assumed JJ and I are trying to outdo Alex Honnold, like that's even possible," he said, absurdity building in his voice. "So now she's always telling me, in front of other people, to *please be safe with all the free soloing.*" He imitated her voice, and it was obvious that Acadia seriously aggravated him. "It's beyond embarrassing. I don't climb free solo. If I get injured climbing, I want to know that I took every precaution and played my part in being safe."

I nodded as he unloaded the truth. "I appreciate you telling me, Sawyer. What about the bicycling?"

Sawyer chuckled and said, "Every year JJ and his mom participate in a bicycle ride to benefit heart disease. JJ's dad died when he was a toddler from heart disease, so doing the ride together is a way he and his mom cope and try to raise money to help with research and stuff. Anyway, JJ trains pretty seriously for it, and he invited me to train with him the last couple months at POGS. I jokingly told him I'd train so hard that he'd eat my dust. He said I'd have to ride over a hundred miles a day to outdo him, and I joked that I would ride all over the country to prepare. Sell my Jeep and bike everywhere. Of course, Acadia overheard the last part and instantly became an expert on my cross-country bicycling plans. Like I know anything about bicycling across the country, though it would be pretty amazing," he said. "So again, Marlee, no need to worry. And yes, Ellie knows that I've been riding with JJ. As much as I'd like to ride with him in the race, it's near his hometown in Tennessee in the Great Smokies the week before our fall semester at POGS starts, so I won't be able to ride with him on race day, but training with him has been pretty cool."

Wow. I couldn't help but feel a twinge of jealousy over Sawyer's exciting life. He had so many adventures going on that it seemed like everything must be fun for Sawyer. "It's really cool that you get to have so many adventures," I told him. "My life sounds so humdrum compared to yours."

"Yeah, climbing a tree to escape a flood is – what did you say? Humdrum?" Sawyer asked.

"Yeah, like monotonous, mundane, typical."

"You're good with words, Marlee," he replied. "Did you ace that lit paper you were working on the day we had our webcam chat?"

"Close enough," I said.

Sawyer laughed and said, "You are *so* not the perfectionist that your sister is! But anyway, you're good with words and Marshall is good with chords. You two could write music together."

"Yeah, I bet it's that simple," I said, doubt etched in my voice.

"You really should talk to him," Sawyer plainly said. "About music, hiking, future plans, anything, but mainly, you need to talk to Marshall about Ellie moving away."

I didn't say anything for a minute.

"Mar-Mar?" he gently, but firmly, said.

"I heard," I said with a sigh. "I'll try."

# CHAPTER 14

I n the next half-hour, my legs went numb. For a painfully long while, I thought they must be on fire. Then it felt like my thighs were being stabbed with dozens of needles and I wondered if that's how acupuncture feels. Then my legs visibly shook and twitched, and I wondered if that's what Marshall referred to when he told me to not get Elvis leg. After that, my legs just felt numb again, which was a welcome relief.

Thankfully the water level was decreasing pretty quickly, and I hoped that in another ten minutes or so we could scoot down and stand on the ground. If my legs would work, that is. It felt like hours that I had been in this position with my feet, hips, and back pressed flat against the trunk of the tree and my knees bent in front of me. I was concerned about how cold Sawyer might be, since he had gotten so wet. "Are you warm enough?" I asked.

"No, but at least the sun is starting to come out. How are your legs and wrists?" Sawyer asked. We didn't have to shout to be heard anymore.

"My wrists are okay, but I think they'll be pretty bruised. My legs are, um, still attached to my body."

Sawyer let out a chuckle and a little groan and said, "We will majorly need to stretch after this."

"Not to be awkward," I ventured to say, "but, uh, how is your bladder?"

"I gotta go," he truthfully said. "Would've been nice of Thad to let us use the 'facilitrees' before handcuffing us."

"I don't think Thad concerns himself with being nice. Customer service is not his forte," I said.

"No kidding. Do you think he *actually* works at a state park?" Sawyer asked. "I thought people needed background checks to work in government positions."

I shrugged. "Maybe his record is clean. And besides," I couldn't believe I was standing up for him, but as I was thinking aloud, I heard myself say, "if this land used to be his grandpa's and he grew up playing in these forests, and now his grandpa is old and confided in Thad about hidden treasure, it makes sense that he would be protective of the cache and the whole area. He wants to make his grandpa proud. He just didn't think about how his strong will to find it fast would affect us. I wish he believed that we don't want anything to do with it. If he wasn't so paranoid, it would be fun to help him find the treasure. Reading that homemade map would be a cool challenge, and we could find the cache and bring it to his grandpa. If Thad was a trustworthy person, that is. Is it illegal to handcuff people to a tree?"

"Ellie was right," Sawyer remarked, and his voice held a glint of humor.

"Hmm?" I asked.

"You do think out loud. Was that rambling or was that conversation? Am I supposed to respond to all that or just listen?"

I laughed.

"But in all seriousness, your idea does make sense. Thad would be protective if he considered this area his grandpa's. Native Americans would beg to differ about *owning* land, but Thad seems pretty self-absorbed and hasn't a clue that not everyone has the same perspective."

"Yeah," I agreed as I noticed that the water around the trunk of the tree was below the grass and only looked a few inches deep. "Can we go down now?"

"Sure, let's take it slow. Start inching down on the count of three," Sawyer said.

I tried to carefully walk my feet down the tree like a squirrel, but I pretty much skidded down, totally out of control, scraping my whole backside against the bark. My sweater scrunched up, exposing my low back to the cold, rough bark. Ouch. I tried not to screech, but I think I did. At least my arms were protected by the sweater.

"Sorry about that!" I said, realizing that my uncontrolled descent tugged Sawyer down too. I hoped I didn't yank on his wrists too hard.

"It wasn't too bad," Sawyer said unconvincingly. He sounded like he was in pain.

Suddenly we heard Ellie's voice calling to us from farther up the hill. "Are you okay?" she sounded worried.

"Ellie! You should've seen it!" Sawyer yelled. "We survived a flash flood! Water was raging against our tree and we had to climb up, handcuffed and all! And your sister saved me, well, both of us, from drowning when a tree branch dragged me below the surface!" I couldn't see Ellie, but I'm sure that Sawyer's announcement wouldn't have boosted her confidence about our plight.

"What?! Let me find a dry path back to you!" she shouted.

"Follow the hill back toward the tent. You should be able to cross the stream near the tent and make it back to us," Sawyer suggested.

"How does she look?" I asked Sawyer, wondering if Ellie looked scared and weary, or hopeful and confident, indicating that help was on its way.

"Pretty," Sawyer said.

*Never mind.*

In a few minutes, Ellie emerged from the trees and explained that the ground was soaked for about thirty feet on either side of the stream. She immediately ran to me and hugged my head, then tugged down my fleece jacket. I was shivering, partly from the chill of the storm and partly from adrenaline surging through my body. Had we really just survived a flash flood?! "Did you see the storm?" I asked Ellie.

"I heard the thunder over here and worried that you might get rained on, but until I hiked over the ridge I had no idea that the stream was flooding. How did you climb up the tree?"

"With a lot of help from God and a ton of grit and determination," I said.

"Aww, Marlee, it's okay to brag up my muscle mass in front of Ellie. She won't be annoyed," Sawyer teased.

"Haha," Ellie's voice lacked humor. "*Obviously* you're strong, but I can't believe you two *actually had to climb a tree while you were handcuffed to it* to escape a flood!" She hugged my head again and looked deep into my eyes. "Are you okay?" she whispered. I nodded.

"Were you able to call for help?" Sawyer interrupted our silent sister conversation.

"Yes, and I have good news and less-good news," Ellie smiled.

"We're listening," Sawyer urged.

"Okay, so good news first: there are two backcountry rangers in this forest who will bring tools to cut the links on your cuffs. The less-good news is that they are now on their way to Thad's location and will probably be arresting him, to make a long story short. But, don't lose heart or bladder capacity, because the other good news is that while I was talking to the ranger with my phone from the peak – which has an amazing view by the way – I explained who I was and the situation, and the ranger said they had just received a call from our parents. Lydie and Marshall are with them, and they are on their way to us in this meadow. Our dads will surely know how to uncuff you," she said all in a rush.

*Yeah, they practice getting out of handcuffs in their spare time,* I sarcastically thought. But *maybe* they could figure out how to get us out. A girl could hope.

She walked around the tree to see Sawyer's face. "Thank you for going," he said. "I'm so thankful you were safe, and that you talked to the ranger. You did great, Ellie."

"To be honest, it was kind of exciting, and I loved having a crucial role in this rescue. And it's *really* good that I didn't know you were in such a near-death experience until after it passed."

Sawyer chuckled, and then in a serious and somber tone, said, "Ellie, I need to tell you something."

"O...kay," Ellie hesitantly said.

"Ellie, please don't think of me as a failure, but I failed a class at POGS and am on academic probation and have to retake Art Appreciation." Sawyer proceeded to tell Ellie every detail he had told me, including the reason he couldn't accept help from the flirty tutor, Acadia. His voice wavered a bit, like he was nervous, but he was honest and laid it all on the table, so to speak.

At the end of his speech, I said, "That was great, Sawyer. I'm proud of you for being honest."

Ellie was silent for a moment. An increasingly long moment. Was she rethinking her potential relationship with Sawyer? Would she still be interested in a guy who failed art? Was she mad that he hadn't told her yet? Why wasn't she saying anything? And then, *finally*, she spoke. "Marlee is right. I'm proud of you for being honest. And I'm proud of you for all the classes you did pass."

"Right!" I interrupted. "Aren't you glad he aced Wilderness Rescue?"

Ellie giggled. "Yeah, that's true. And really, Sawyer, nobody can be perfect at everything. So you have to take the class again – it's not the end of the world."

Did Ellie just say that? "Wow, Sis, you're making great progress as a recovering perfectionist."

Sawyer and Ellie chuckled, and Ellie replied, "Well, if *I* had failed Art Appreciation, I wouldn't have the same positive outlook. But I'm not disappointed in you, Sawyer. Surprised, since you're kind of a perfectionist yourself, but not disappointed. If you need help coming up with essays about the art, I can email you a powerpoint I made a couple years ago that summarizes some well-known pieces and various interpretations. Maybe it'll give you some essay inspiration. You'll be fine, Sawyer," Ellie encouraged.

The much-anticipated conversation went smoother than anything else on this trip, and I was happy that Sawyer got the burden off his shoulders. Then Ellie quietly said, "I have wondered if you have too much on your plate-"

"A plate of food sounds great," he said.

"You know what I mean, Sawyer," Ellie gently chided. "So you're on trek, which is super busy, and you can't really study much then. When you're back at campus, you're a full-time student with a part-time job at the climbing gym, and you're biking with JJ along with additional workouts. And with church and studying and hanging out with JJ-"

"You're right," Sawyer sighed in resignation. "I'll cut out biking and have more time for studying this fall. JJ won't need me to ride with him until next spring."

Well, it was a start.

"Cool," Ellie said.

Then I heard Sawyer whisper something to her. All I heard was "...tell....figured it out....you....her."

*Here it comes,* I thought. Ellie's turn to spill the beans. Stupid messy beans that would change my life. Our life.

Sure enough, I heard Ellie take a deep breath as she stepped over to face me. "Hey Sawyer, can we sit down?" I quickly asked. My legs still burned like crazy, and now my heart rate was picking up again in preparation for Ellie's official news statement informing me – the *last* to find out – that she would be moving.

"The ground is soaking wet," Sawyer reminded me.

"Oh yeah," I stammered, "silly me." I made myself face Ellie. She gave a slight smile and began, "Marlee, remember when I told you about that wildlife vet tech internship in Idaho?"

*Duh, how could I forget? It's all you talked about for like three weeks. Please don't talk to me like I'm just an acquaintance.*

Not wanting to be rude, I nodded. She said, "Well, about a month ago I received a call from the admissions counselor who congratulated me on being chosen to take the opportunity of a lifetime."

I forced a smile that didn't reach my emotions, but I let her keep talking.

"I immediately prayed about it and talked to Mom and Dad. Obviously I wanted to go, but I wanted to make the best decision. I called Sawyer and even talked to his parents, and discussed it with Lydie and-"

*W-w-what?* "Wait, you told Lydie and Mr. and Mrs. Miles, but you didn't tell *me*?" That hurt every bit as bad as my back scraping down the trunk of the tree.

Ellie gasped. "Marlee," she paused, and she broke eye contact. After a minute, she said, "I couldn't tell you. Leaving you will be the hardest part of moving to Idaho. You're my best friend, Marlee. I needed to get advice from-"

"Everyone besides me?" I pointedly asked. "If you really thought of me as your best friend, why didn't you tell me right away?" I bit back a sob. Why did I keep crying in front of Sawyer – er, around Sawyer?

Ellie was silent. Sawyer gently said, "Marlee, when Ellie called me to say she had been offered the position, she wasn't jumping for joy. Even though she had prayed for it, the first thing she said was, 'I don't know if I should go. Marlee and I are so close, and I don't want to leave her.' And the reason Lydie knows is because she was in the kitchen with your parents when Ellie answered the phone when the admissions lady called. Ellie asked your parents and Lydie if she should accept the position and asked them how they thought you would take the news."

That explanation was somewhat soothing. I gulped down the lump in my throat. "I know that you've prayed a lot for God's guidance, Ellie," I said masking my heartbreak with a little more confidence, "and I think that since the door has opened for you to be a part of the wildlife vet tech program, that you should take it. I mean, if you think about it, if you weren't supposed to go, they probably wouldn't have offered you the position, or some other obstacle would have gotten in the way." I believed what I had just said, but it sure would be hard to say goodbye when she moved. I looked away from her face.

She placed a hand on my shoulder. "I agree," she quietly said. "And we are going to keep up our evening talks," she assertively said. "We are going to call every night and keep each other fully informed of everything."

I nodded with a half-smile. I was hungry and tired and sad. And no matter how much Ellie tried to convince me that my opinion mattered in her decision, she had accepted the position without talking to me. And that burned.

# CHAPTER 15

E llie draped out rain clothes next to the tree so we could sit and rest our exhausted legs. Sawyer and I scooted down the trunk of the tree, both of us moaning as our legs collapsed. I winced as I stretched my legs in front of me. If muscle fibers could talk, mine would scream for mercy and organize a riot. Stretching my legs in front of me felt a lot better, though. Next Ellie took off Sawyer's and my hiking boots and set them in the sun to dry. Then she retrieved our sleeping bags to wrap around our chilled bodies. After that she dug out a backpacking stove and cooked some alfredo noodles and chicken from a foil pouch for us. I don't remember having to be spoon-fed as a little kid, so it was very strange to have Ellie bouncing between Sawyer and me, hand-feeding us food. But the food was warm and satisfying, the flood had receded so the stream was about ten feet away from us, and we chatted easily with each other while we waited for Marshall, Lydie, and our parents. It was strikingly peaceful compared to the previous hours.

Ellie offered to hold water bottles for us, but we both politely declined. We were thirsty, but didn't want to add any fluid to our already strained bladders!

Something else was bugging me, and I needed to think, so I started to talk. "Sawyer, did you see the deer? The buck who could barely keep his antlers above the surface of the flood?"

"I caught a glimpse of him."

"Do you think he survived?"

"I really don't know, Marlee," he said. Ellie just listened as she squatted to the side so that she could see both of us. Then quietly, he said, "Realistically, he probably drowned."

"That could have been us."

"I know. It's pretty humbling. In some ways we're so strong, but in the grand scheme of life, we're pretty delicate too," he said. "Just a couple minutes without air or a blow to the head, and we'd be goners."

"For some reason, seeing that deer struggle for his life, to fight with all his strength to take another breath, really got my attention. From our perspective, it seemed like he didn't have much chance, but he continued to fight. He wasn't giving up for anything. That's real tenacity. To fight fiercely with every ounce of strength for what needs to happen – in that case, to get air. But maybe that's what God wants from us – to use all our strength to do what's right and to follow His commandments. This world we live in swirls around us and rushes past, like the flood. It tries to drag us into the current. But we have to keep our heads out of the water, keep our eyes on the prize of the upward call, and keep living God's way," I said.

"We need to stay grounded to our tree," Sawyer offered.

"Yes! As long as our tree is firmly rooted in God's Word." I smiled.

"That's an interesting point, Marlee," Sawyer said. Ellie nodded in agreement. "Actually, it's a great analogy. And it's even more meaningful to us since you actually used every ounce of your strength to pull me back up when the tree dragged me underwater."

Ellie's eyes grew huge. "So you didn't say that just to scare me?"

Sawyer humbly said, "I was petrified. I thought we would both go down. And then Marlee heaved against the tree and yanked me back. It's probably a miracle our wrists didn't break. She saved my life. With God's help, of course."

Speaking of wrists, mine were starting to bruise and had looked and felt swollen since the moment I had fought to pull Sawyer back up the tree. I figured that his wrists hurt just as bad.

"That's amazing," Ellie murmured. "I'm so sorry you two are in this dilemma. It makes me so mad at Thad knowing that his impulsive, paranoid, freakish ideas almost caused your deaths."

I knew what she meant. We wouldn't have almost died in the flood if Thad hadn't handcuffed us here. Sawyer interrupted my thoughts. "Yes, and I don't condone what Thad has done. But something Marlee said got me thinking. Maybe Thad doesn't have parents who have taught him how to treat people. Maybe he and his grandpa need the money from the treasure just to pay bills. It might be that Thad just doesn't know how to be respectful."

"True," Ellie agreed, "but he is an adult and if he has a full-time job at a state park and knows how to talk to all of us like a civilized person, then he must be pretty aware of his thoughts and actions."

"Yeah," Sawyer said, "made in God's image but tainted by the devil."

"That reminds me," Ellie nervously said, "um, can I ask you a question?"

"Sure," Sawyer said, "as long as it's not about Claude Monet."

"Nope." Ellie giggled, and then seriously said, "When we heard Thad on the phone with his sidekick, what he said about me was nauseating. Is that how guys really think about girls? That girls are just bodies to have 'fun' with?"

Sawyer was quiet for a minute before he uncomfortably said, "Don't let Thad make you think all guys are evil. Many guys do think that way, yes. And I agree that it's nauseating. I think most Christian guys struggle to keep their thoughts about girls pure, but thankfully God helps a lot. Problem is, so many guys these days don't care about God or even people and just think about what feels good and what is fun. As a Christian, I try to avoid tempting situations and definitely pray that God will help me to treat you, and all girls, respectfully."

"Thank you," Ellie murmured.

"And anyway, I need to stay on your dad's good side," Sawyer said, and I could picture his teasing face on the other side of the tree.

"*Somebody* is confident about my dad's opinion," Ellie teased.

"Your dad has always been crazy about me." I could hear that Sawyer was grinning. "It only took me a long time to get on *your* good side."

I laughed, and Ellie tilted her head and slyly smiled. "True."

Ellie blushed. They were perfect for each other.

"So, I take this to mean that you two aren't going to live together before you're married?" I asked hopefully.

"Definitely not!" "No way!" their voices choroused.

"Good. I'm glad you are going to take the high road," I said. "Lydie and Marshall and I need all the good role models we can get."

"That's cool that you care about that, Marlee," Sawyer said.

"I think it's cool that you care about it too," I replied.

Ellie was noticeably silent before she quietly asked, "Did you even consider for a moment that I would live with a guy outside of marriage?"

I shifted my weight, partly because I was uncomfortable physically, and partly because of the look on Ellie's face. She looked completely let down with my question. "Umm, no. I mean, no, I didn't think either you or Sawyer would compromise your commitments to purity. It just seems like you and I have, uh, not talked as much recently. The wildlife vet tech program was kind of a shock, and then when that meant you'll be moving to Idaho, only half an hour from where Sawyer goes to school...I wasn't sure if anything else had changed too."

Ellie looked troubled. After a breath she proceeded, "Marlee, this past year has been one of the most fun years I've had with you. Staying up late together and talking with you has been remarkable. I wouldn't trade that time for anything. You'll always be my sister, and I truly hope we can always be close. The reason I held off on telling you was because I was trying to figure out how to tell you."

"I would've rather heard it from you than through the grapevine."

"I'm not the grapevine!" Sawyer protested.

"You know what I mean," I politely argued. "Ellie, I would've been more excited if you had run up to me as soon as you got the call and hugged me and jumped up and down. I would've celebrated with you. Before crying. This way, I just feel so left out. Like I was the last to find out about this life-changing news you have." I shrugged away a tear.

Despite the still soggy ground, Ellie knelt right next to me and wrapped her arms around my shoulders. We hugged as best we could and softly cried together for a minute. "Don't think the distance will come between our talks, Marlee. Or our closeness. And this program is only for eighteen months, and the experience I'll gain will be so beneficial for my studies. I'll tell you all the details on the phone. And we still have six weeks together to make awesome memories and prepare. And in my absence, you and Lydie will have the opportunity to grow closer just like you and I have. You'll do just fine, Marlee. We'll both do well in our new experiences. And I'll be a phone call away when you need me."

Her pep talk was comforting, but part of me knew things would never again be the same. Sure we could try to call, but inevitably, we wouldn't be able to talk every single time we tried. She would be busy with her internship and new friends at the program, and my life would continue as usual, minus Ellie. *Sigh.* I would just have to make the most of the rest of the summer with Ellie. And then try to keep on living as normally as possible after she left me.

"If I may interrupt," Sawyer's voice broke my train of thought, "Marlee, you're right that life changes. It can be bittersweet, but try to view these changes as opportunities for growth. Every time you leave your comfort zone, you grow, and that's exactly what God wants for you. This is an opportunity for you to grow and be the big sister to Lydie that Ellie has been to you."

He made sense, but I couldn't help but want to cry out that it seems like I've done a lot of leaving my comfort zone in the past year or so. I had dug out of a snowy would-be grave, hiked on an empty stomach, fought off an aggressive bear, helped carry my injured sister, taken an AP Literature course that nearly ruined my sanity, given a speech about the layers of the atmosphere, rock climbed in the dark with no safety gear, climbed a tree in the dark with a nutjob chasing us, and been handcuffed to the same tree during a flash flood. Why would God pick *now* to have my sister move halfway across the country?

"Marlee," Sawyer's voice gently cut through the silence. "You need to talk to Marshall. He'll be able to encourage you, and I know that you can trust him. He would never try to hurt you like that Bentley guy. Talk to Marshall."

*How does he read my mind?* "Okay," I managed to say. Ellie patted my knee and stood up.

Just then, we heard Marshall's excited voice ring out, "Their camp is right over – whoa, the stream is humongous!"

Ellie sprinted off toward the direction of Marshall's voice. "OVER HERE!" she yelled.

I was instantly grateful that our group would all be together, but before everyone arrived, I had to say something. It was now or never, so I blurted, "Sawyer, thank you so much for talking me through this. And I definitely don't think of you as the grapevine. You're the big brother I always dreamed of having."

"Thanks, Mar-Mar. I'm here for ya'."

"I know. Thank you."

Our families came jogging over to us at the tree. For a moment everyone gaped, taking in the unexpected sight.

"What happened?" Marshall and Lydie cried at the same time.

In the next few seconds everyone seemed to talk at once. "Who did this to you?" my dad demanded.

"Did they hurt you?" Mr. Caleb asked, noticing the large cut on my face.

"Why did they do this to you?" my mom angrily asked as she gingerly touched the area around my cut.

"Why did you let them handcuff you to a tree?" Ms. Julia asked in bewilderment, rushing to Sawyer's side.

"Was it Thad?" Marshall and Lydie demanded.

Dad dropped to his knees in front of me and started touching my face and shoulders and asking if anything hurt. Mom turned on her cell phone, presumably to call for help, but shoved it back in her pocket when she saw it had no service. Then she joined Dad in his search for broken body parts. Meanwhile, Lydie and Marsh circled the tree with wide eyes.

Finally Sawyer shushed the crowd. "Marlee and I are safe and healthy, and while we appreciate your concern to give us more water, our bladders are plenty full. Ellie climbed the peak to get enough cell phone service to talk to the rangers. They're on their way to cut the handcuff links. That will be after they find, investigate, and detain Thad, which is also a high priority. So if anyone can break our handcuffs now, our bladders would be greatly appreciative."

I couldn't help but giggle at Sawyer's explanation. Our parents were aghast at this most unusual situation, but based on Sawyer's speech, the biggest concern was our full bladders.

"But what happened?" all four parents cried in unison.

"Marlee, I never expected you to wind up in handcuffs with my bro," Marshall teased. "Figured if it ever happened, I'd at least be involved." I playfully rolled my eyes and shook my head at him. I didn't even try to suppress my grin.

"Let Sawyer and Marlee explain it all, since I slept through the first scene and was absent for most of the second," Ellie said.

Seven pairs of eyes crowded close to us, mouths tight in anticipation of the story.

"Well, after Marsh and Lydie left in search of you," Sawyer began, "I sent the girls to the tent to sleep while I kept vigil out here. Just in case Thad or his sidekick ventured into this meadow, I wanted to guard the girls."

*Aww, how chivalrous.*

"Before too long, Marlee came over to talk since she couldn't sleep. So she and I were right by this tree talking when we saw someone's headlamp shining around the meadow. She climbed the tree-"

"In the dark!" I pointed out. "I've had several opportunities to climb in the dark in the last twenty-four hours!"

The guys chuckled and the ladies grimaced before Sawyer continued. "She's good at it, too. So she climbed the tree, and I pretended to be asleep in the grass. When Thad came over and shone his light on my face, I pretended to wake up and even talked like JJ to confuse him and make him think I wasn't me. It didn't take him long to recognize me though, and he realized that it's my blog that apparently has sent droves of people into this very forest looking for *his* treasure. He was ready to body slam me and go harass Ellie in the tent when Marlee sneezed and came down. Thad convinced himself that Ellie had gone with Marsh and Lydie, and *maybe* he believed us when we assured him that we wanted nothing to do with his cache. Well, he must not have fully believed us, because in a heartbeat he had us handcuffed to the tree like this."

"But that's not even the best part!" I said. "So here Sawyer and I sat, waiting for Ellie to wake up, and then after she left to call for help it started to get really dark. A big storm blew in with wind and lightning and thunder and crazy heavy rain – *so* glad it didn't hail. And while it was raining we started seeing a bunch of animals running up the ridge. I thought it was totally cool until Sawyer told me to look at the stream. That slow-moving mountain stream from last night had swelled into a raging flood that was rapidly approaching our tree. We had no choice but to push our bodies up the trunk of the tree by pressing our feet and backs into the bark. We inched ourselves up about eight feet to escape the water."

Sawyer said, "But then, while we were hunched up there waiting for the water to recede, a tree branch jostled by and got tangled around my boot. It dragged me away and under-"

"And Sawyer didn't answer me, and all I knew was that my wrists felt like a team of horses were pulling on them. Thankfully God helped me not go under the surface of the water-"

"And Marlee saved my life," Sawyer concluded.

Then our parents really looked aghast. Mom ran her fingers through my hair and gently pressed on my wrists. *Ouch.* Her prodding reminded me of the dentist jabbing the poker into my gums to see if my wisdom teeth were close to emerging yet. I wanted to yelp in pain, but my wince was enough to make her stop. Meanwhile, our dads looked around the meadow and studied the stream for a minute before returning their attention to us.

"And when I found them," Ellie went on, "I covered them with sleeping bags to help them retain body heat. But as you can see they both have slightly blue lips. They need to get into dry clothes."

Ms. Julia had her hand over her mouth and slowly shook her head in shock. My mom put her hand on Dad's arm and said, "What are we going to do?"

"We'll figure something out," Dad said and Mr. Caleb nodded. "Can you ladies help them warm up? Caleb and I will try to break them free."

Mr. Caleb and Dad went in search of a rock and a hatchet while our moms started a backpacking stove to warm water. We reminded them that we didn't want water, but they explained that they could fill a couple water bottles with warm water to nestle next to our bodies. That sounded cozy. Lydie squatted next to me while mom and Ms. Julia worked with the water bottles and wrapped an arm around my shoulders. "That is a phenomenal story," she said. "I'm so proud of you, Marlee."

I looked at her, noticing how grown-up she looked. Had she really just said she was proud of me? Maybe I could fill a similar role for her that Ellie did for me. I smiled at her and said, "How was your hike? Did you see Thad? Did you enjoy being on a rescue mission with Marshall?

Did you get rained on? Are you hungry? You must be exhausted. Were the night sounds and scenes amazing?"

She giggled and said, "The hike was pretty cool. I knew we were in a precarious situation and had to hurry, but it was actually awesome, and I enjoyed it. Hiking next to the stream was so pretty. We didn't see or hear Thad, and other than stumbling into the stream, we stayed dry."

My eyes widened and she said, "We didn't get rained on, but yeah, I was going a little too fast over some rocks and slipped right into the chilly water. I didn't want to scream or make noise, but the water was shockingly cold, and I kind of yelped. But Marshall hustled over and helped me out. I'm glad I had dry clothes along or I would've gotten *so* cold. And yes, I am tired. I'm so tired that I might just lay my head on your lap and sleep," she lightheartedly said.

"Help yourself." I smiled. "Warm me up."

In just a minute though, Dad and Mr. Caleb had returned. Dad had us lower our arms all the way to the ground, which meant Sawyer and I had to scoot our bodies forward and lean back. Then Dad wedged a couple rocks between the links of our handcuffs and the ground, making sure our hands were as far apart as possible. Mr. Caleb wound up his arms with the hatchet, held his breath, and then stopped just before I was going to close my eyes. "Forrest, will you pray for this? No way can I swing this at our kids without asking God for help."

*Phew.*

Dad said a little prayer, thanking God that we were together and mostly safe, and he asked for God's all-powerful help with the handcuffs.

Mr. Caleb looked more confident this time, but our moms did not. Dad stepped back, Mr. Caleb made eye contact with Sawyer and me and told us to hold absolutely still.

"No sneezing now, Marlee," Marshall teased. I couldn't help but smile.

My hand gripped the grass until my knuckles were white. A few small chainlinks away, I could see Sawyer's hand in a similar position. "Hold off on the jokes, Marsh," his dad said. Lydie held her hands over her mouth and her eyeballs were about the size of ping-pong balls. I didn't know whether to watch or close my eyes, so I opted to keep my focus on the chain links where the hatchet would hopefully strike. And try not to scream.

I held my breath and sensed Sawyer tightening too. Everyone was silent. Mr. Caleb's arms were still extended above his head and after what felt like an eternity, he swung his arms down with tremendous force. The blade of the hatchet struck the exact center of the chain links. Everyone let out a huge breath, but when Sawyer and I tried to pull our arms apart, we realized the links hadn't broken. Instead, Mr. Caleb's force had driven the rocks several inches into the ground.

"Would you look at that!" Dad observed.

"The ground acted like a shock absorber." Mr. Caleb rubbed his whiskered jaws and contemplated for a minute.

He and Dad surveyed the soggy ground and realized they could hammer rocks into the dirt all day before the metal links would break. "I'd like to get my hands on the thug who did this to you." Dad squeezed his fists.

"Forrest, let's control our anger if we can," Mom said. "We need action, not anger. Did the ranger give any indication of how long it might be before they could get here?" Mom asked Ellie.

Ellie shook her head. "It all depends on how long it takes to get Thad out of the wilderness and into a police car."

"Could we pick the locks?" Marshall asked. Mr. Caleb shrugged and said it was certainly worth a shot. Dad still looked mad.

"Too bad he didn't use the toy handcuffs with the safety latch," Lydie muttered, which made me laugh.

Marshall grabbed a knife and set to work between us. He tried several tools on his multipurpose knife. He furrowed his brow and studied the locking mechanism, gently moving our hands to accommodate his work space. He prodded the skinniest tool into the keyhole and wiggled and twisted it around. After a minute of that, he tried again with another tool. He probably spent about ten minutes fiddling with the four locks before his cheeks blazed red and he gave up. "Sorry. I tried," he mumbled.

"We're glad you did," I said.

Sawyer quietly agreed, but he sounded like he was dozing off. Lydie was half asleep on my lap, and if not for my full bladder, I would've slept too.

# CHAPTER 16

I must have dozed off for a while though, because what felt like a minute later, Mom gently shook my shoulders. "Sweetie, the rangers are here."

*Awesome!* I opened my eyes and saw two uniformed backcountry rangers talking to Dad and Mr. Caleb and Ms. Julia. Marshall and Lydie were already standing by them and listening intently. When the taller ranger looked my way, he gave a reassuring smile and strode over. "Quite the character you encountered. My name is Ranger Douglas, and that's Ranger Rose. You must be Marlee?"

I nodded and offered a grateful smile. "Thank you so much for coming."

"I'm so sorry you had to go through this. We've been trying to catch up with Thad for about six months now. We've received reports of him mildly threatening other hikers, but this is by far the most drastic action he's taken, at least to our knowledge. You can be proud of your sister for calling us with his coordinates. You won't need to worry about him anymore."

I smiled as Ranger Rose approached. She nodded and smiled at me and said, "I'm Ranger Rose. We were shocked to hear what had happened to you and, is it Sawyer?" she nodded toward Sawyer.

"Yes, I'm Sawyer."

Ranger Douglas, whose skin was as dark as JJ's, took off his backpack and began unpacking it. "We searched Thad for the keys to the handcuffs, but we didn't find them. This is Plan B." He showed us a handheld tool with a circular blade. "It's a battery-powered angle grinder. We'll cut the links so you can move freely again. When we arrive back at the station, we'll call a locksmith and get you fully freed from the handcuffs. Any questions?"

"How do you know we're innocent?" Sawyer plainly asked.

The two rangers exchanged a quick grin, and as Ranger Douglas knelt down to look at the chain links and clean the dirt off them, Ranger Rose said, "Thad admitted to handcuffing you to a tree for personal greed, and he said you had not harmed him."

"And you believed *him*?" Sawyer critically asked.

Ranger Rose laughed. "We deal with very little criminal activity here, mostly underage drinking and poachers. If you two were criminals who Thad wanted to turn in, he would not have abandoned you without contacting authorities. His behavior indicates that he is the criminal."

Ranger Douglas said, "And before you woke up, we were able to talk to your parents for several minutes. You seem like a credible bunch. Criminals don't have a support group like this, and Ellie probably wouldn't have called us for help if you two were the troublemakers. That would be self-incriminating. Besides," he added with a smirk, "real criminals can usually get out of handcuffs."

That made our dads exchange a grin. Mr. Caleb laughed. "I'll admit, this was the first time I've had to try to break handcuffs." He turned to the rangers. "For the record, I couldn't do it."

This time the rangers laughed. Then with a camera they snapped a few pictures of Sawyer and me, for documentation, they explained. *Great, such a flattering angle. And unwashed, unruly hair to top it off.* "Alright, just hold your hands on the ground and keep the chain taut while I make the first cut," Ranger Douglas instructed as Ranger Rose helped hold each of our wrists. My wrists were increasingly sore from when Sawyer was nearly dragged away, but I told myself to focus on how close we were to freedom. Lydie and Ellie came over to cover our ears, which was really nice of them.

It took about ten seconds of Ranger Douglas's bulging muscles operating the angle grinder to cut a metal link. For a moment I just stared at our wrists with the chains dangling. Freedom! The rangers walked to the other side of the tree to cut the links of the other pair of handcuffs. Again Ranger Rose held our wrists steady while Ranger Douglas made the cut. When we were free, Sawyer and I stiffly stood up, letting our sleeping bags fall to the ground. Then we hugged each other. I can't really explain why, other than to say that we had been through an insane trial together and felt victorious, so a hug made sense. Next my parents and sisters hugged us, and I even found myself offering Ranger Rose a hug. I wiggled my eyebrows at Marshall when Sawyer and Ellie's hug lasted like ten seconds. He laughed and elbowed Sawyer in the ribs. It was my turn to laugh when Sawyer released Ellie and pulled Marshall in for a bear hug. Ranger Douglas shook both our hands and said he was happy to shake our freely-moving hands and have a real introduction.

I said "thank-you" about a dozen times before Sawyer and I scampered off in opposite directions to relieve our screaming bladders.

Upon returning to the meadow, the rangers told us that we needed to change into dry clothes and eat and hydrate before hiking back to the station. Sawyer and I took turns in the tent changing while our families prepared food and water for us.

When we all convened around two backpacking stoves, Mr. Caleb offered a prayer of thanksgiving. That was expected, but it grabbed my attention when he also prayed for Thad. At the conclusion of the prayer I noticed Ranger Rose quirk an eyebrow at Mr. Caleb, who was already busy scooping food into bowls for Sawyer and me. There was enough food for all of us, but I sure appreciated being served first. The others in our group had eaten recently, and they hadn't gotten wet from the storm that hit Sawyer and me. I smiled at my mom, who beamed back at me.

Ranger Rose said, "I guess that's another sign you're not criminals."

Several of us glanced at her questioningly.

"When we detained Thad and later his sidekick, they certainly weren't praying for you all. You really care what happens to him?"

I saw my dad swallow like he does when he's mad but trying to chill out. I can always tell because his Adam's apple bobs and he sniffs his nose just once. After a moment of silence, Dad shrugged. "Well, he's made in God's image, too. We're all guilty of sin. I don't feel compassion for him like I do for my family, but as a person, I can care about him. He's somebody's son and made his mother proud when he was born, though it's hard to believe now."

Mr. Caleb nodded. "Right. As rangers, if he had been injured or ill, you would be obligated to rescue him even if he was breaking the law. You'd care to help him simply because he's a person."

Ranger Rose laughed and said, "Let me tell you, rescuing your family is much more enjoyable than working with him."

"Well I hope so!" Lydie quipped.

Everyone chuckled before Sawyer addressed his dad specifically, while still speaking to the whole group. "Dad, you said something interesting. Did Lydie and Marshall tell you the part about how we helped Thad when he was dehydrated and overheated? And then he turned on us and chased us out of 'his territory.' He would've roasted to death if we hadn't helped him. Then when he became a threat to us, I almost wished we hadn't helped him. But you and Mr. Forrest think we did the right thing to help him?"

I was listening closely while gently rubbing my wrists where the handcuffs had bruised them. I was glad to be able to wiggle them around a bit and not be as constrained as when we were still connected. Even though I was trying to massage away the pain, my eyes were fixed on our parents and their reactions to Sawyer's question.

"Yes, I think you made the right choice," Mr. Caleb responded. Our moms nodded in agreement.

"What if we had known he would later threaten us?" Marshall asked my next thought.

After a minute of quiet consideration, Ms. Julia answered. "What keeps coming to my mind is that as Jesus was dying, He prayed for the people who killed Him. Based on that example, I would say that even if you had known Thad was a criminal, you were right to offer him first aid – carefully, that is."

We all nodded in silence as we let the weight of the matter settle in our minds. It was difficult to wrap my mind around, and one glance at Ranger Rose told me she was puzzled by our reasoning. Ranger Douglas was silent but appeared confident as he reached in his pack for a notepad and pencil.

He had a string of questions for us kids, starting with the time and place we first met Thad. As the storyline progressed, his questions were primarily targeted at Sawyer and me. Every detail, from finding the hand drawn map and overhearing Thad's phone conversation, to him yelling at us on top of the ridge, and eventually handcuffing us, was relayed. Rangers Douglas and Rose listened closely, taking plenty of notes and murmuring things like, "What else do you remember?" Our parents listened in wide-eyed silence.

Finally Dad joked, "I'm a little jealous that you kids keep having these adventures. Next year let's stick together for any and all treks we take!" Did I mention that Lydie gets her happy-go-lucky sense of humor from Dad?

After the questioning, the rangers gave Sawyer and me quick medical evaluations, just to make sure we were strong enough to hike back to the ranger station. We both passed, but they said I would need to wash my cut twice a day with filtered water while on trek. I was glad Sawyer's soaked clothes hadn't given him hypothermia. It was a blessing that Ellie arrived when she did and covered us up with sleeping bags to retain as much heat as possible. Our boots weren't one hundred percent dried, but good enough that with our spare socks on, we should be able to hike in them.

After we packed up Sawyer's tent and the stoves and were all set to hike, we followed Ranger Douglas down a trail we hadn't hiked yet. We walked in no particular order, but after a few minutes of settling into our own comfortable paces, I found myself in the rear near Ranger Rose. I smiled at her and thanked her again for rescuing us. "I don't think my bladder could've lasted much longer."

Ranger Rose laughed heartily and said, "I am very impressed with your families and how you all handled this unexpected happening."

"It sure was unexpected. I never like when our group needs to split up, but this time it was necessary. Thankfully we've all hiked together enough that we work like a well-oiled machine. We're a pretty strong team," I said with a shrug.

"A very strong team," affirmed Ranger Rose. "You're some of the most prepared, equipped, and experienced hikers I've ever helped, and I've been a backcountry ranger for almost ten years."

I beamed at her for her positive observation, and in reply she said, "You know who you remind me of?"

"Who?" I was curious.

"Recently, I don't recall exactly when, but within the last year or so, I read some articles and saw a news report about a bunch of teenagers who hiked into the path of an avalanche. It was down in Colorado. According to the reports I read, the kids managed to build a snow shelter, avoid hypothermia, and properly evacuate one of the kids in the group who had suffered a broken leg in the accident. Those kids hiked themselves to safety. Their story made a big impression on me. I'd love to meet them someday."

I gaped at her before I spluttered, "You heard about us?"

Ranger Rose stopped short and stared at me. "That was you?" We both looked stunned for a minute before we resumed hiking.

I thought it was my turn to talk so I said, "It might be the same story. Last summer, we five kids-" I hesitated to tell the truth to an experienced ranger who might think less of us, but it was too late to stop spilling the truth, so I continued. "Well, we made the somewhat reckless decision to summit a peak at night during a full moon. We kept our itinerary secret from our parents. And yes, we were swept up in an avalanche. Lydie, my little sister, broke her leg, and Marshall and I couldn't hike to the ranger station because I had a pounding headache since I was dehydrated and there was a stick in my head-"

Ranger Rose looked perplexed, so I said, "Yeah, a small stick had forced its way right into my forehead. You can see the scar here." I pointed before continuing with the story. "So we hunkered down in a snow shelter and the next day Sawyer taught us how to build a stretcher out of a tarp and sticks and we carried Lydie to the ranger station. I've never been so exhausted or hungry in all my life!" I recalled.

As I relayed the story that was so ingrained in my memory and my life, Ranger Rose stared at me in wonder. Just when I began to think I should confess my mindlessness to go along with the moonlit summit plan and try to convince her that none of us were usually bad kids, she opened her mouth and said, "The story amazed me. When I read it, I thought to myself, 'Those kids have tenacity. The world needs more people like them who can problem-solve and cooperate and fight pain to achieve a greater good.' I can't believe I've had the opportunity to meet you."

I suddenly felt embarrassed and said, "This is only the second time I've needed rangers to help me. I'm not normally a problematic kid. You probably think teenagers these days are horrible, but honestly, we didn't intentionally provoke Thad or try to stir up trouble."

Ranger Rose shook her hands in front of her to stop my self-criticism. She gave a little laugh and said, "Quite the contrary, Marlee. I am beyond impressed with you and everyone in your group. Did you hear when I said that your tenacity, problem-solving, and cooperation inspired me? Marlee, after I read your story, Ranger Douglas and I, along with two other rangers, started planning an outdoor program for youth. We plan to tell your avalanche story to our participants and give them hypothetical situations, a realistic supply of gear, and time to figure out a plan. We've been accepting applications from interested teens for six weeks already. Our first class starts next week."

It was my turn to gape. "Really? That is so cool," was all I could think to say. I hadn't thought of our group as inspirational. I figured we had set an example of what not to do, but I hadn't considered that we had set a good example for how to recover from a bad situation.

"Marlee, I can't believe I didn't put the clues together sooner. I was so busy thinking about Thad's information, that I didn't notice you five were the group I've been longing to meet!" Ranger Rose said. "I'd love to have you talk to our participants. When is your family leaving Montana?"

"We have to leave this weekend," I said disappointedly. All good things must end.

"Hmm, would you consider participating in a brief interview that we could record to show our students? If each of you five could explain a survival tip that you used, or give details on the first aid you administered, or share anything that helped you get through, that would be invaluable to our program."

I thought for a minute and nodded. "Yes, I'd be happy to," I agreed. "I can't speak for the others, but I think they'll be cool with it too."

"Excellent! And thank you, Marlee. It's truly great to meet you," Ranger Rose said.

To think that a youth program was inspired by our survival story nearly made me stop in my tracks. In my mind, I returned to the evening that I agreed to do the moonlit summit. Never had I dreamed that a year later, I would have the opportunity to teach others how to reach safety in the wilderness. It struck me that last summer's off-itinerary hike could accomplish something great. The avalanche had not been on *our* itinerary, but God could see the big picture all along. The realization excited me and touched me deeply.

# CHAPTER 17

When we arrived at the ranger station, Ranger Rose explained her plan to all of us. Our parents agreed and had to sign release forms for those of us younger than eighteen. While we waited for the locksmith to arrive, Ranger Douglas and Ranger Rose took turns filming our interviews. They asked each of us a couple of different questions, and they excitedly said they would have about twenty minutes of footage to include in their lesson plans. They also took a photograph of the five of us lined up, and they said that Sawyer's and my dangling handcuffs in the picture would give them another lesson plan!

I'd never before felt like a celebrity, but the rangers acted like we were renowned. They kept asking us details of our avalanche survival story and taking thorough notes, like everything we said was priceless information. After we had exhausted the topic, they moved onto more questions about our experience with Thad, where the rangers again applauded our responses.

We asked about Thad's treasure, and whether the land had actually belonged to his grandpa. Ranger Douglas cast a wary look at Ranger Rose and said, "Well, we're not at liberty to give personal information. However, we can say that yes, Thad's grandpa is a former owner of some of the land that is now within this protected forest. He was afraid that if his health would fail and the need for him to move into a nursing home would arise, that the land may be divided up in a way that displeased him. For that reason, he signed the land to the state forest with the agreement that it would always be protected from developers. As far as the treasure, it looks like he was also accurate about that report. For now, we've alerted the police who will begin an investigation."

Ranger Rose continued speaking, "Different states have various laws regarding hidden treasure and whether the finder or the landowner actually owns the treasure. There will be many steps to take before we know all the facts surrounding Thad's treasure. Until we give you the all-clear or you hear about it in the news, please keep it quiet. The last thing we need now is mobs of greedy and no doubt, unprepared, people prowling around. It's quite possible that the courts will rule that the cache does indeed belong to Thad's grandpa and after paying taxes, they may be able to retire on a cruise ship. After Thad serves his time for harassing you, that is."

Just then the locksmith arrived. He stepped in the door and introduced himself. Ranger Douglas stayed by our sides and explained the situation while Ranger Rose went to talk to our parents. I was so eager to be de-cuffed that I didn't listen to their conversation.

"Well, I'll be," the locksmith said. "I'll tell you kids, I've been a locksmith for longer than you've been alive, and I've seen some mighty unique scenarios. This about beats all, though. Handcuffed to a tree through a flash flood? I'll be," his voice trailed off as he visually inspected Sawyer's and my wrists. "Of course I could use a key, but that's not nearly as fun, and since the handcuffs are already nonfunctioning with the chains cut, we might as well keep this interesting. Follow me out to my mobile workshop." Like ducklings, our whole group, rangers included, followed the locksmith outside.

I read "Right on Key Locksmith Services" on the side of his full-size van and he opened the side doors, revealing a warehouse of tools and equipment. "Gather around, audience," he said. Sawyer and I stepped into the workspace inside the van. Our families and the rangers crowded by the door to watch. There were cabinets running down the length of the van with a workbench in the center. Attached to the wooden workbench was a bench vise, like my dad has in the garage. He placed a stool near the vise. "Ladies first," he gestured to me to sit on the stool and told me to extend a forearm. He lined up the handcuff on my left wrist between the jaws on the vise and secured the cuff in place.

We were all curious to see what he would do, and everyone outside the van was nosing their faces in to watch. Marshall seemed especially interested as he peered right over my shoulder. The locksmith chuckled and gestured to Marshall. "See I was like you, always taking things apart, curious to see the inside. Drove my Ma nuts, but I sure learned a lot!" At that point he pressed what he called a tapered punch onto a rivet and popped the punch with a hammer to drive out the rivet. "One down, a few more to go," the locksmith grinned. He repeated the process with three more rivets on my left wrist's cuff. As soon as four rivets were removed, the whole handcuff fell apart and the locksmith poked a wire into the inside to retract the ratcheting locking wheel. He narrated the steps as he performed them, which was informative to all of us. Marshall said he was taking notes in case I wound up in handcuffs again. I rolled my eyes but told him I appreciated his thoughtfulness. Ranger Rose took a few more pictures of the lock-smith at work, for the judge, she said.

When the locksmith released the lock with the wire and took the pieces of the handcuff into his own hands, my hand felt wonderfully light and mobile. My wrists still felt swollen and bruised, but I wasn't complaining! I held up my right hand and he went to work, again securing the handcuff in the vise, then popping out several rivets with the tapered punch and hammer. When it was time to manipulate the ratcheting locking wheel, he passed the wire to Marshall and offered him a turn.

Marshall blushed but accepted the offer and wiggled his way into the van. "There's a first time for everything," he said. Even though he had closely observed the locksmith, it took Marshall a minute to release the lock. He grinned as the pieces of the handcuff fell into his hands.

I quirked an eyebrow and said, "Now they have your fingerprints." Marsh laughed and thanked the locksmith for letting him have the chance to break a handcuff.

He nodded and said, "Next up is the gentleman."

Sawyer and I swapped places and the locksmith again narrated his steps, mostly for Marshall's benefit. He said due to liability, the only step he would let Marshall perform was the last step of using the wire to release the lock. Within ten minutes, Sawyer was de-cuffed too.

"Freedom," Sawyer sighed happily as he extended his hand to the locksmith for a firm shake. "Thank you, sir, for using your skills and equipment to help us."

The older man laughed and said, "It's my job. Happy to help."

"What do you normally do with locks and broken handcuffs?" Lydie wondered aloud.

"Completely disassemble it and save any good parts, or I keep fiddling with the mechanism to better understand the lock. Or I give it to my grandson so he can play with it. When it has totally outlived its purpose, it gets sold as scrap metal." I never knew locksmiths were so interesting and knowledgeable. I sure was thankful that he had put his skills to work on Sawyer and me!

"How much do we owe you for your services?" my dad asked the locksmith as he stepped out of his van.

"Let's say fifty-five dollars. Two customers, a ten-mile drive to get here, and use of my tools. Your politeness and the fact that you were victimized gets you a little break on the cost. Any less than that and my wife will roll her eyes at me," he said with a chuckle.

Dad and Mr. Caleb both dug in their backpacks for their wallets to split the cost. I didn't have my wallet with me on trek, but I quickly told Dad I'd pay him back when we got home. Sawyer said much the same to his parents. Before the locksmith left, I ran over to shake his hand as Sawyer had done and to thank him. "I sure am glad you took stuff apart as a kid and knew just how to help us today, – I didn't catch your name," I said.

"Call me Roz." He grinned. "And you're very welcome. Enjoy the rest of your hike, and if you find yourselves handcuffed again, you know my number." He pointed to the side of his van. He talked to Mr. Caleb and Dad for another minute, getting signatures and filling out documentation. He said he would attach his files to the ranger's and, along with the pictures they took, there should be adequate evidence against Thad.

Relieved to be free from restraint, I hugged my mom, then Ellie, then Lydie, then Dad, and finally Sawyer. Marshall and I did a fist bump, and he told me I was the rowdiest girl he knew since he'd never had a friend handcuffed before. We both laughed.

Ranger Douglas smiled and said, "Well, folks, what's next on your itinerary? Your backcountry permit is still valid through the weekend. If you're up to heading back into the wild, we'll let you be on your way." We followed him as he began walking back inside the ranger station.

We exchanged glances with one another, and my mom said, "Our kids almost died!"

"Again!" Ms. Julia, who was standing beside my mom, looked equally unsettled. "All of this treasure hunting, handcuffing, and flood drama makes me think we should play it safe."

"Yes. I hate to cut our trip short, but given the circumstances-" Mom began.

"With all due respect," Ranger Douglas interrupted, "the criminal is gone. You don't need to worry about Thad anymore. And the weather forecast looks clear for the next week."

"Really, Mom," Sawyer said, "what *else* could go wrong?" Marshall and I laughed, but Ms. Julia raised an eyebrow and gave us "the look" that made us stare at the ground.

"Would you feel better if the rangers help us plan our new itinerary?" Mr. Caleb asked his wife.

"Are we the only ones who think this is weird – to walk right back into the danger our kids just escaped? Marlee and Sawyer nearly died!" My mom said.

Ranger Douglas solemnly said, "I understand this is a lot to take in. The decision is yours, of course. Just know that Ranger Rose and I can assist you if you like." He stepped behind the counter and started typing something.

"Quinn," Dad gently said as he put his arm around Mom's shoulders, "this is our last chance for a family trip before Ellie leaves home. I know you're scared. Believe me, when Marshall and Lydie told us what was happening, I was terrified. But the big danger is past. Can we try again and finish this summer's trip on a good note? We'll all be together." At the close of his rebuttal, I caught Marshall's eye and smiled. Marsh discreetly pumped his fist, expecting a victory. The thing is, Dad and Lydie can convince my mom to do almost anything, and Mom can convince Ms. Julia to do almost anything.

Mom looked at me and then Sawyer and asked if we felt up to more backpacking.

"I've never felt more up to it," Sawyer said, and I bobbed my head in agreement. Sawyer spoke again, "Marlee and I can easily hike three more miles to a campsite for tonight. Supper will be a little late, but you wouldn't want to miss this chance, would you, Ms. Quinn?"

*Marlee and I? Easily? Three more miles? Umm, is he exaggerating?* I squeezed my lips shut and smiled. Sawyer's enthusiasm for the wilderness was contagious.

Mom looked skeptical, so I said, "We should try to get one more family selfie on a peak before Ellie moves."

Mom slowly nodded, and then all four parents talked for a few more minutes amongst themselves. I eavesdropped, and the conversation tipped in our favor. My parents and Mr. and Mrs. Miles stepped to Ranger Douglas's counter. Ranger Douglas smiled and said, "Did you make a decision?"

Mr. Caleb said, "We'd like to get back to nature, but this time we'll stick together." Then he, Sawyer, Marshall, and my dad pointed to the topographic quadrant map on the counter and began planning, conferring with Ranger Douglas about trails and campsites.

Ranger Rose stepped over to my sisters and me and, making eye contact with each of us, she said, "Girls, it's been a pleasure to help you. I just want to mention that if any of you are interested in pursuing a career as a ranger, I'd absolutely write a letter of recommendation for you." With that, she handed each of us a business card with her contact information, and she thanked us again for the interviews for their students with the youth outdoor program. "And anytime you are back in this area, we'd love to have you speak to our students. Please keep in touch with Ranger Douglas and me. You seem like the type of kids who will continue finding yourselves in unique situations. We'd enjoy hearing about them."

We smiled back at her and I took a long look at the business card she had handed me. I began to wonder if maybe I could someday become a ranger like Rose. When I looked up from the business card, Sawyer caught my eye from across the room and gave me a nod and a half-smile, like he knew exactly what I was thinking. I smiled back at him and mouthed, "Thank you." He gave a wink and another smile before turning his attention back to the map. I tucked Ranger Rose's business card into the top pouch of my backpack where I would easily keep track of it – just in case I ever needed a recommendation.

Right then, Mom came over and wrapped her arm around my shoulder. "I'm so thankful for another happy ending, Marlee. I think I felt a gray hair sprout when I saw you handcuffed to the tree. Although I must say, since you were secured to Sawyer, that kept my anxieties in check."

I giggled and said, "If you had seen us in the flash flood, you might've sprouted half a dozen gray hairs!"

She shuddered but then teasingly said, "Good thing we were on the sunny side of the mountain at the time then, isn't it?"

I laughed again.

Our dads and Sawyer gestured us all over to the counter where they were studying the map. Dad said, "We're talking about taking the trail right here by the ranger station to Loren's Meadow," Dad dragged his finger across the map, "and spend tonight there. It's really close, so we could do it even after all that's happened today."

Mr. Caleb said, "Then tomorrow, weather permitting, we can climb the peak and see what Ellie already saw."

Ellie smiled. "I'd love to see it again. With my group!"

Sawyer pointed on the map. "And then Thursday we'd like to hike up the ridge and check out a glacier over here."

"That sounds great!" I said, along with the affirmation of everyone else in the group.

We turned to smile again at Rangers Douglas and Rose. "Happy trails," they said in unison.

"We'll see you in a few days and hopefully not sooner," Dad said. We loaded up our backpacks and filed out the door of the ranger station. Mr. Caleb and Sawyer led the way to the trailhead and we fell into our own comfortable paces. Dad, Lydie and Marshall were just behind Mr. Caleb and Sawyer, then Mom and Ms. Julia, with Ellie just behind. I was in the caboose, but I didn't mind being last. The warm air felt perfect, the fresh air had that crisp mountain air scent that I love, and the birds were singing. Surrounded by my family and friends and knowing that creepy Thad and his sidekick were out of the forest, I felt content about the hike to come. No, I was more than content. I was stoked.

I gave a little skip and hustled to catch up to Ellie and match her pace. I linked my arm through hers, and she looked at me curiously. "Enjoying your freedom?"

"Definitely," I laughed. "Hey," I said seriously, "you were pretty brave to hike alone to call the ranger station. I know it was super risky, and you were probably scared, but I'm glad you did it for us. It was really cool of you. It made me feel really proud of you, Ellie."

Her eyes glowed at my praise, but she was silent for a moment before tentatively asking, "You're not even mad that I hadn't told you about the wildlife vet tech program?"

"No. When I found out that Sawyer and Lydie knew before I did, I was hurt. After you and Sawyer explained why you hadn't told me yet, I understood, though. I mean, I felt left out, but it's not about me. It's about your big news." I tried to remind myself not to be selfish or have a pity party. "And it's great news. It'll be a great opportunity for you. I'm happy that your dream is coming true." The more I said it, the more I believed it. *Just hold back the tears, Marlee.*

Ellie stopped to hug me and said, "I was going to tell you."

"When?"

"I had planned to tell you on our last morning here, so that way you could grieve the end of the summer's backpacking and my move at the same time. I know how crying always gives you a throbbing headache, so I wanted to condense the pain for you."

"That was...thoughtful," I replied.

Ellie sheepishly said, "I know this is going to be a massive change for both of us. And I'm going to miss you like a hot dog misses its ketchup. I figured we could both cry the whole way home from this trip, and then not feel so sad when I actually move."

I nodded and quietly said, "Next time you have big news, you can tell me right away. I don't need a perfect pre-planned announcement. Just hearing it come from you would be nice."

Ellie nodded and said, "I'm sorry. I didn't want to hurt you." I could tell she was biting back tears, and I decided we had adequately covered the topic of her upcoming move.

To lighten the mood, I nudged her with my elbow and said, "Hey, we still have one thing on our summer to-do list."

We made eye contact and grinned. "The Stanley Sisters Peak Pirou-ette," we chorused. It's a little dance move we invented several years ago, and it's our top-of-the-mountain tradition. None of us can really dance, but it's fun and always makes us laugh. As usual, we could hardly wait.

# CHAPTER 18

We hiked until my leg muscles reminded me of what they had endured that morning. The scenery was amazing with the soaring evergreen trees, towering peaks and bright blue lakes. But when my legs started to feel like cooked noodles – that I didn't cook – I desperately hoped we were near Loren's Meadow and could rest.

"Just another quarter-mile," Dad encouraged us. My dad always means well when he encourages us, but sometimes it's so disheartening when he says "almost there" and it turns out to be two more hours of hiking. But I could probably make another quarter-mile. To occupy my mind on something other than my burning muscles, I decided to pray. Sometimes – okay most of the time – my prayers feel scatterbrained. Not beautifully eloquent like Lydie's. It's like my mind is a web of thoughts and just when I start to tell God about one thing, I remember that I'm supposed to ask that He'll heal somebody, which reminds me to be thankful for my current health, which reminds me to pray for the malnourished little kids around the world, which – ugh! I'm such a scatterbrain sometimes!

So I started with thanking God profusely for keeping Sawyer and me safe and for reuniting our group. And then I thanked God for Roz, the locksmith, and somehow, in my scattered conversation with God, I had a thought: It's time to forgive Bentley and Sierra. *Whoa, where did that come from?* I remembered that Sawyer had brought up Bentley's name when we were handcuffed to the tree. I guess that planted the seed in my mind. Ugh, I didn't like thinking about Bentley and Sierra. It made me feel all fired up and, well, left out. But I couldn't shake that thought: It's time to forgive Bentley and Sierra.

I took a deep breath and looked around. The rest of my group was still hiking and chatting as if nothing monumental had just happened. I honestly felt like a smothering weight had been lifted from my shoulders. But *could* I forgive Bentley and Sierra? Just like that? Bentley had known I liked him, and he had sure acted like I was the only girl he knew existed. And Sierra had cheered for me when he asked me to dance. She had arranged so we would sit by each other at the bonfire and help each other assemble s'mores. And then when I saw Bentley and Sierra together holding hands at Here's the Scoop, I felt like my heart was a galloping horse, and my stomach was being tied in a knot. They were laughing, and when I watched him slip his arm around Sierra's shoulders, my throat felt like a boa constrictor was strangling me – or at least what I imagine that would feel like.

How could I forgive them? Why should I forgive them? It was stubborn of me to not forgive them. For as long as I could remember, Dad and Mom taught us the importance of forgiveness. Dad would remind us of the endless times God forgave His people in the Bible, and Mom would tell us that Jesus says we are expected to forgive just the same. That's why I needed to forgive them. It was the right thing to do. There was no denying that.

Sure, I should be cautious about trusting them in the future, but I shouldn't keep holding the past against them. I guess I hadn't even realized that I hadn't forgiven them, but based on how free from the old pain I felt right then, I knew that I had finally overcome the hurt they had caused me. A smile spread across my face as the realization set into my mind.

"Penny for your thoughts?" Marshall asked.

*Whoa, how long had he been by my side?*

"Hey Marsh," I said, trying not to sound surprised. "I haven't asked you how your and Lydie's night hike was."

Marshall grinned. "It was pretty cool, Marlee. I felt like an undercover ranger or something. It was all mysterious how we were sneaking next to the river. It also made me think about the slaves who had to run away from the plantations at night. I thought of how daring they were, and desperate, which was sad, but I tried to focus on the emergency at hand. And it's good we didn't know you were handcuffed, or we probably would've panicked and hiked too fast and gotten hurt. It was a good level of suspense for us."

I smiled. "Cool. Lydie kept up well?"

"Yeah, she's a strong hiker. I still think of her as so young and last year with her broken leg, I didn't see much of her hiking. I kind of forgot she grew up during the year, you know."

I nodded. "I know what you mean. She's one of us big kids now."

Marshall chuckled, and a minute later said, "I'm a little jealous that you and Sawyer got to survive the flash flood together. It's not that I want any of us to go through a flash flood, but since you did, I kind of wish we all could have been part of it."

I glanced at him and he hurriedly said, "I know that probably sounds weird. But like last summer, we all made it through the avalanche together and then we hiked out together and our group is really strong from that." He shrugged. "It would've been another cool adventure for us all."

"I get what you're saying, Marshall," I answered. "And I'm a little jealous of the hike you and Lydie took. But I'm sure last night won't be the end of our adventures together."

Our eyes met and we did a fist bump. A moment later he said, "It's cool that our parents always arranged these backpacking trips for our families. I hope we can always have these trips."

"Me too."

The next thing I knew we were setting up our tents in a beautiful meadow sheltered by a majestic mountain peak on the north. The sun in the west made the mountain face glow an amazing golden orange color. I couldn't help but stare for a moment. I even tried to capture a few shots on my camera, but as usual, the photos didn't reflect the incredible view my eyes saw. I guess I can scratch photographer from my list of potential careers. This incredible mountain view would have to be a picture for my memory.

I set to work helping Ellie and Lydie pitch our tent. After draping a tarp on the grass, we arranged our tent on top and pressed metal stakes from the corners of the tent into the soil. Sometimes it's really hard to get the stakes into the ground, especially without bending them, but this ground was ideal for camping and the stakes didn't bend or make us mad.

Then we tossed in our sleeping pads and sleeping bags. Ellie ducked into the tent to line them up. Lydie and I just let her do that step, because in the eyes of a recovering perfectionist, we might not get it quite right.

I took that moment to hug Lydie and tell her how proud I was of her. "I have you to thank," she said, confusing me.

"What do you mean?"

Her face said, "Duh," and her voice said, "Marlee, last year when you and Marshall hiked off to be my heroes, I decided I wanted to be just like you."

Her plain statement took me back. I never knew that. "I completely admire you for being brave and strong that day. Last night when I had the chance to do what you had done last summer, I was so excited. I wanted to make you proud. I wanted to show you how much I look up to you as my big sister." Her words tugged my heart and all I could do was hug her tightly.

Finally I managed to say, "Lydie, you have no idea how much that means to me right now."

"I think I do," Lydie quietly said as Ellie stepped out of the tent and joined us. "It's not that I want Ellie to leave, but I want a friendship with you like you have with Ellie." My heart broke, realizing we had inadvertently left out Lydie. "Don't feel bad, Marlee!" Lydie quickly added. "But maybe if you're ever lonely after she leaves, you and I could talk and laugh after bedtime?"

"Of course, Lydie," I said as I pulled her into another hug. Ellie wrapped her arms around both of us.

"Aww, sisterly love," Sawyer's voice broke into our moment. "I hate to interrupt, but I have a delivery for Marlee." I grabbed the water bottle he handed me as he said, "Your dad mixed up extra electrolytes for you and me to help our muscles recover."

"Thank you!" I emphatically said. "Any chance you can deliver a hot tub too?" I teased.

"Hey now, you know that our muscles need ice, not heat," he playfully chided.

"Yeah, yeah," I laughed.

"Besides, do you have any idea how long of an extension cord we would need for a hot tub out here?" he joked.

"I wonder where the closest hot spring is," I said.

"Doesn't matter, Marlee," he said in his mock-chiding voice.

"We need ice," we said at the same time with a laugh.

"So, should we dangle our legs in the cold river?" I wondered.

Sawyer and Ellie looked thoughtfully at each other before Sawyer answered, "I kind of think due to the circumstances, we might be better off to hunker down and keep dry and warm."

"I agree," Ellie voiced. "While the icy water would help with swollen muscles, you don't need to risk hypothermia for a *second* time today."

Ellie, Lydie, Sawyer and I walked toward our parents who were taking turns setting up their tents and cooking supper. Ellie and Lydie offered to help, and Sawyer pulled me aside. "I really want you to talk to Marshall," he whispered in my ear.

I nodded and took a big breath. "I know. We could go filter water together?"

"Perfect plan," Sawyer said. "I'll get him now." I gathered up everyone's empty water bottles.

In a minute, I was walking with the Miles boys down a rocky slope to the nearby river. It was only about two hundred feet from the campsite, just down the hill from our tents. It wasn't the same river that had flooded. This was called the Pierre River, and it was clear and pretty. I found a spot on a large flat rock that stood above the river about two feet. I crossed my aching legs pretzel-style, and tossed the foam buoy into the clear mountain water. I grabbed a water bottle and twisted the lip onto the bottom of the filter. Without even needing to think, I began raising and lowering the pump handle and watched the water course through the ceramic filter and slowly begin to fill the first water bottle.

I was content to sit and filter water without conversation, but after a half liter had been filtered, I looked up and glanced toward Sawyer and

Marshall. Sawyer met my gaze and gave a meaningful nod. He stood up and said, "I'm going to bring this water up for the cooks." With that, he was up the trail lugging the five-gallon collapsible water tank. Water used for cooking doesn't need to be filtered since it would get boiled, so he was able to simply submerge the water tank and let it fill relatively quickly. And just like that, he had left me alone with Marshall – with whom I was scheduled to talk.

It's not that I don't enjoy a good conversation with Marshall. Earlier on trail, when he talked a lot by his standards, I had fun talking with him. It's just that I was nervous about the conversation regarding how to adjust to life with Ellie a thousand miles away. I sighed, causing Marshall to glance at me. He wordlessly arched his eyebrows before looking back to his own filtration. So much for hoping he would start the conversation! I knew Sawyer wouldn't come back. He purposely arranged for this opportunity. Marshall and I had to filter ten liters of water, which would take a good long time. I wondered if Sawyer had given him a heads-up about the talk.

I liked Marshall. Overall he and I got along really well. Why was I delaying the simple question of "Hey, any pointers for me when Ellie moves? And by the way, tell me about your band."? *Oh, right.* I was afraid of letting myself get any closer to Marshall in case he and I would have a fallout like what happened with Bentley. I didn't want to repeat the pain or to lose Marshall's friendship.

Suddenly I was reminded of my recent realization that I could move forward with life. No more hard feelings at Bentley and Sierra. Furthermore, why should I hold that against Marshall? I took a deep breath. "Marshall, can I ask you a question?"

He made eye contact with me and nodded. Though he was quiet, he looked like he was in a good mood. When I didn't say anything he said, "Say that again, Marlee. I didn't hear you."

I teasingly stuck out my tongue at him, and to my surprise, he lifted the filter's hose and buoy out of the water and walked over to me. Dropping the buoy back into the water, he sat down next to me on the big flat rock. For a quiet minute he simply resumed lifting the water filter's handle up and pressing it down. We listened to the rhythm of the water falling into the water bottles and didn't say anything. But after a minute, he gently elbowed me. "You were saying?"

Without really thinking in advance, I blurted out, "Can we always be friends? Can I always count on you?"

Marshall turned his upper body and squarely faced me. He searched my face and whispered, "What's wrong, Marlee? You seem so troubled about something."

"I just found out Ellie is moving away at the end of summer."

He nodded, and since he didn't act the least bit surprised, I realized that even Marshall had known before me. But he kindly said, "That must have been hard news for you to take. Especially after the somewhat traumatic handcuffing and flash flood." He held my gaze and said, "It'll be a big change, Marlee. But you'll adjust and do well. I know it's hard to believe now. But you'll be busy when Ellie leaves, and the weeks will tick by and before you know it, she'll be on break and come home and drive you bonkers again. You'll help her with her laundry and talk half the night and you'll feel recharged when she departs again. You'll be okay."

"Is that how it is with Sawyer now?" I sniffed.

"You know, sometimes I think Sawyer and I talk more now than we did when we shared a bedroom."

"Really?" A well of hope filled me.

"Yeah, but we're guys. We didn't usually stay up half the night talking about cute guys and bedroom curtains." As usual, his corny joke made me laugh. "He almost always calls me from every peak he climbs. He texts me when he gets back to base camp, he sends me funny pictures of him and JJ, and he even mailed me a birthday card. Can you believe it? Even though he's states away, I almost feel closer to him now than when we lived under the same roof. Who knows? Maybe it will be the same for you and Ellie. Her moving away doesn't have to be bad."

Both of our water bottles filled at nearly the same time, so we were silent as we unscrewed the full bottles from the filters, replaced their lids, and screwed on the next-in-line empty water bottles. We continued pumping the water filters. I glanced at Marshall and studied him for a minute. "So, can we always be friends? Will you always be there for me?"

Looking at me, he assuredly said, "I sure hope so. You're one of my best friends." Then after a minute he smiled. "See, we're best friends, and we live hours away."

I nodded, but I also knew that even though Marshall and I had been bonded by our backpacking and survival experiences together, it's not like we were two-peas-in-a-pod close. I knew there was a significant distance, that we had very separate lives. And it made me feel a bit melancholy, especially when I considered that Ellie would make new friends whom I didn't know. "Sawyer said you play in a band?"

Marshall grinned. "I'm pretty good at guitar these days. My buddy Flynn is teaching me drums too.

"That's cool! I wish I would've stuck with an instrument," I said.

"It's not too late to pick it up again, or learn a new one," he encouraged. "What would you like to play?"

"What would I be good at?" I wondered.

"Can you sing?"

"In the shower." I laughed.

Marshall laughed too. "Lots of famous singers sing in the shower. Have you ever had vocal lessons?"

"Nope."

"It's not too late to start. And you could learn any instrument you want to play. Especially with the internet. There are tutorials for almost everything. And when we get together to plan trips, we could jam and practice together."

I smiled at the thought. Marshall seemed much more carefree than he had last summer, and even than he had when we climbed the ridge. I decided to ask what the change was. "You seem happier than before."

He smiled and sighed. Then he slowly nodded and finally answered, "Hiking last night to get to our parents taught me something. This might sound weird to you, since you're a girl and girls' brains obviously operate on a different wavelength than the rest of humanity." I laughed. He remained straight-faced. "But when Lydie and I got to our parents' site and alerted them of the trouble, I felt like I was good enough. Like I had it in me and was capable of being the hero. I've always lived in Sawyer's shadow, but last night, when I successfully led Lydie through the dark forest, both of us fighting exhaustion, I felt like–" and then he stopped, blushing.

"That's not weird," I encouraged, "go on."

"Well," he quietly said, "I almost felt like a man, like Sawyer. If hiking through the night was an initiation, I had passed and I was in. It made me think I graduated from being a little guy to being a man." He broke eye contact and looked down before murmuring, "I haven't told anyone that. Please don't make fun of me."

"Marshall, I think that's awesome! And I can totally see why that accomplishment means a lot to you. You don't need to be embarrassed at all," I reassured him. "In fact, sometimes when I recall last summer, I wish you and I could have made it to the ranger station the day we set out to reach help. To be the heroes would have been awesome. But it worked out well in the end that we all went together. Anyway, we all admire you and Lydie for making it to our parents last night!"

He smiled at me and said, "So you do understand?"

I nodded and smiled right back. "You rocked it. I was a little jealous, to be honest."

"Yeah?" he asked.

"It sounded like fun to sneak through the dark next to the river, ready to fend off wildlife and bandits. I bet our folks were all pretty stunned when you two showed up at their camp," I said.

"Oh yeah. Your dad was taking down the bear bag when we ran in. My parents weren't up yet. And your dad did a double take and just stared at us, all red-faced and sweaty. He ran over and hugged Lydie and asked me what was going on. When we told him everything, he shook my hand and said I did 'real good.' Then I woke up my parents, and Lydie and I helped tear down their campsite while your parents made breakfast. My dad even said he was proud of me." Marshall's face glowed as he recounted the praise, and I was genuinely happy for him. We bumped knuckles, and I told him I was glad to know a real he-man. I thanked him for keeping Lydie safe and said I was proud of him too. He appreciated it, but it was clear that the praise from his dad meant the most to him.

"Oh, before I forget," Marshall said. "Don't tell Lydie I told you, but she really looks up to you. In fact, she told me that *you* are her hero."

"She did?"

Marshall nodded. "I wanted to tell you. Since you're going to be the only big sister in the house soon, you should know that you've already got a fan who wants to be just like you."

*Wow. I guess I had better take up an instrument and study hard in school and work out all the time and help Mom and Dad and actually be someone worth looking up to.*

Apparently Marshall read my mind, because he quirked an eyebrow and said, "Marlee, that's good news. I don't think it means you need to change anything you're doing. Lydie looks up to *you*, not some checklist of accomplishments. She admires the way you treat people. And it meant the world to her when you and I hiked for help last summer. Just keep being the best person you can be, and you'll do great." With that, he patted my shoulder and said, "And yes, we can always be friends, and I'll always be here for you."

For a moment I wondered if Marshall and I would ever be really close like Sawyer and Ellie. The thought gave me a flutter of excitement and I felt myself blush. Marshall noticed my blush and grinned. Maybe he was wondering the same thing. We fist bumped, and even though neither of us knew what the future would bring, we knew we had true friends in each other.

# EPILOGUE

M arshall had been right about the time flying by since Ellie had moved for her wildlife vet tech program. The night before her departure, in a bittersweet, spontaneous sister ceremony, she had given her lime-green bean bag chair to me, charging me with the Big Sister role and formally inviting Lydie to come to me for late-night talks. We hugged and cried and said good-bye, and like Marshall had said, in a few months that passed like a blink of an eye, there we were, ready to reunite.

Over the years we had visited the Miles' home a handful of times, but this was to be the first time that we would have Thanksgiving together. Normally our families just got together with our own physical families, in various places around the Midwest. It was a change, but I was actually really excited to spend the weekend with our backpacking family. Dad is closer to Mr. Caleb than some of his real relatives. And besides, Grandpa and Grandma were along, also very eager to see Ellie again. I sure was looking forward to spending time with my grandparents and Ellie, regardless of the location.

My grandparents had ridden with us from Wisconsin to the Miles' cozy house in Iowa. After plenty of planning and airfare searching, it was determined that the easiest way for Sawyer and Ellie to spend time with their families for the long weekend was to take a direct flight from a city close to POGS and the wildlife vet tech program to the city nearest the Miles' home. We had been informed that the flight was on time and that Mr. Caleb and Marshall had returned with Sawyer and Ellie about forty-five minutes ago. I could hardly wait to see her.

Lydie and I linked arms with each other and with Grandma as we walked toward the door. Unexpectedly, I felt butterflies in my stomach when I caught a glimpse of Ellie through the bay window. Several people and a dog greeted us at the door.

"Happy Thanksgiving," "Welcome," and "Come in," all chorused from inside the house. Ellie beamed and took turns hugging each of us. When it was my turn, she whispered, "This weekend, can we please talk late?" I nodded into her shoulder and savored the familiar smell of her leave-in conditioner.

Ms. Julia called out a welcome but looked a little frazzled with kitchen preparation, so Mom and Grandma rushed in to help her. Mr. Caleb was peeling carrots and handed Dad a paring knife, pausing long enough to shake Grandpa's hand. While working with the raw veggies, Grandpa, Dad and Mr. Caleb all started talking about a new hiking boot that was supposed to be more lightweight than previous models.

Meanwhile, Sawyer and Ellie instantly started showing Lydie pictures of POGS and different animals that Ellie had helped treat. "Marlee, hon, good to see you!" Ms. Julia called. I smiled and asked if she needed help. "Thanks, dear, but I think we'll manage now. You go have fun." I began to raise an eyebrow in question – everyone had a job and was having fun. What was I to do? Just then, Marshall nudged my elbow and led me to an adjoining room that he simply called The Band

Room. Arranged around the room was a variety of instruments, and on the walls were several framed pictures of mountain scenes, most of which I recognized. Seeing memories of our mountain adventures brought a smile to my face.

He grabbed a guitar and strummed a few chords and handed me a harmonica. I laughed and said, "You know, once upon a time I played piano and violin." It's true. I hadn't kept up with my lessons, which I regret, but maybe I could remember some. Maybe I could even resume lessons.

"You know how to play piano and violin?" His eyes grew huge and he pointed to an electric keyboard. "Let's make some music, Marlee."

I plunked out a simple song I remembered on the keys and he said, "You've got potential. Let's jam."

*Here goes nothing,* I thought as I attempted a chord while Marshall played like a semi-professional. Lydie skipped in and asked what she could play. Without stopping his strumming, Marshall called out, "Drums or vocals." I glanced to the corner and sure enough, there sat a drum set. *Mr. and Mrs. Miles must wear ear plugs when all the instruments are being played.* With a confidence that I envy, Lydie sat behind the drums and started rat-a-tatting on the snare drum. At least, I *think* that one is called a snare drum.

In a few minutes, everyone was crowded in The Band Room and I heard a few different melodies and conversations going on simultaneously. Dad and Mr. Caleb were onto the topic of tents, Mom and Ms. Julia were talking about slow-cookers *(yawn)*, and Sawyer and Ellie were telling Grandpa and Grandma about their new adventures in Idaho. I caught Marshall's eye and we smiled. Behind his face, I saw the photo of us five kids that Ranger Rose took before Roz broke Sawyer's and my handcuffs. Recalling the moment and the day, I felt eyes on me. Glancing around, I realized that Sawyer had caught me staring at the picture. He gave me a knowing smile and a wink. Seeing Sawyer and being reminded of what we'd been through was momentous. I knew then that I had changed and grown since our handcuffing experience.

Four months ago, I was being chased by a lunatic and a barrage of anxiety regarding the future. I was so wrapped up in my worries and first-world woes that I was oblivious to the flood that nearly overtook Sawyer and me. Something about surviving a flash flood and a potentially violent person had changed my perspective. I needed to let go and let God. Now, free from the handcuffs and the fear, I could smile with confidence knowing that God would always make my paths straight as long as I kept my trust in Him. And I was very thankful for my family and friends to share the journey with me.

# About the Author

*Photo Courtesy Krista Swanson, ©Simple Wonder Arts*

Liz is the author of the Off the Itinerary series, the wife of a professional tree climber, and the homeschooling mom of three energetic and laundry-producing children. Liz once spent a summer in Colorado teaching rock climbing, which she believes was a fantastic way to make money and memories. She resides with her family in Wisconsin, where they enjoy hiking and rock climbing. Liz and her husband have also backpacked in Colorado and the Grand Canyon, which have provided inspiration for her writing. She makes adventurous stories to encourage others to find adventures and expand their comfort zones (though admittedly, she still needs lots of practice expanding her own comfort zone).

For book discussion guides, please see https://mlizboyle.com/

# Acknowledgements

Writing *Chased* has been a blast! It has only been possible with the support of God and Christ, and with support from my husband Dustin, with whom I really did sprint through a cobblestone downtown with our arms full of rented ice axes to beat the parking meter. I'm thankful to my parents; my priceless beta reading team for pouring their energy into fine-tuning *Chased*: Nia Flavin, Marie Gibson, Miranda Gibson, Hannah Gilmer, James Guy III, David Markopoulos, Cynthia Saladin, Jennifer Saladin, and Abigail Shafer; my thorough editor Beth Jernberg; my children for giving me daily adventures; and each of my extended family members and close friends for encouraging me;

With very special thanks to my real-life locksmith friend, "Curly" Chris Orozco, for undauntingly and extensively answering my many, many questions about the details of locksmithing.

To adventure seekers everywhere, this story is for you.

# DEAR READER

Dear Reader,

I hope you enjoyed *Chased* as much as I enjoyed writing it. One of the best ways to help an author is by word of mouth. If you liked this adventure, please tell your friends about it (and check out *Ablaze*)! Posting reviews online is another great way to support authors. The more readers that find this story, the more I can keep writing adventures for us all to enjoy!

Adventure is everywhere. Read it. Live it. Share it.

Liz

# EXCERPT FROM ABLAZE

"M. Liz Boyle tackles the topic of showering difficult people with grace and forgiveness, making this a must-read for Christian teens. Adventure seekers who loved *Avalanche* and *Chased* will fall head-over-heels for the adventure that heats up in *Ablaze*!" - author Allyson Kennedy

***

This summer the Stanley sisters and the Miles boys are excited to hike together again, and now they have the unique opportunity to help two of their ranger friends with an outdoor program in the beautiful Montana mountains.

Marlee has always considered herself a willing follower. Give her a direction and she's happy to help. Her older sister Ellie is a natural leader, and Marlee is content in her role as assistant.

Marlee and her sisters have been assigned to help with Ranger Rose's team, and they are savoring the adventure. But in a heartbeat while the group is divided by a few hundred feet, fire breaks out between Ranger Rose and Marlee's group. In this enthralling finale to the Off the Itinerary series, Marlee must face her fears with courage that only God can provide.

***

A month ago I would've jumped at the chance to help lead OutPro. I would do almost anything for the rangers who rescued us, and this chance was practically a dream come true. But that was before. I really did want to make Ranger Rose proud, but I felt unworthy of her confidence in my ability to lead. I was so out of my comfort zone, and I was only kidding myself to think I could make the rangers proud and contribute to OutPro. Braelynn and Shelby had shown me that I wasn't up to leading. I'm just a hot mess – a hot mess who is almost in tears. And how could Ranger Rose be so delusional to think I could be helpful? I couldn't stand to see disappointment in her face, so I looked down and scratched a bug bite on my shin.

Sure, I signed up to help lead. But at this point, I decided OutPro would be better off if I just tagged along. I would participate just enough to stay off the Rangers' radar, but not so much to be annoying and divisive. Because lately when I try to lead, bad things happen. And in a forest that was reportedly ready to burst into flames, I did not want to be a leader.

www.ingramcontent.com/pod-product-compliance
Lightning Source LLC
Chambersburg PA
CBHW032007170626
46807CB00006B/2695